MOON IS COTTON & SH

A Short Fiction Collection by Tracy DeB-

To Henry & Elaine ...
& the Best Connemara
Lamb In The World
Tracy DeBrincat

REVOLUTIONARY
MAMA

CONNECT. SUPPORT. INSPIRE.
REVOLUTIONARY - MAMA.COM

Subito Press ★ Boulder, Colorado ★ 2010

Subito Press is a nonprofit literary publisher based in the Creative Writing Program of the Department of English at the University of Colorado at Boulder. We look for innovative fiction and poetry that at once reflects and informs the contemporary human condition, and we promote new literary voices as well as work from previously published writers. Subito Press encourages and supports work that challenges already-accepted literary modes and devices.

2009 Competition Winners

Fiction: Tracy DeBrincat, *Moon is Cotton & She Laugh All Night*
Poetry: Stan Mir, *Song & Glass*

Subito Press
Boulder, Colorado
www.subitopress.org

© 2010 by Tracy DeBrincat

Library of Congress Cataloging in Publication
Data available upon request

978-0-9801098-6-3

Generous funding for this publication has been
provided through an Innovative Seed Grant from
the University of Colorado at Boulder, and by
that university's Creative Writing Program.

Grateful acknowledgment to the editors of
the following publications in which these
stories first appeared, sometimes in different
versions: "Glossolalia" in *Whiskey Island Magazine*;
"Superbaby Saves Slugville" in *North Dakota
Quarterly*; "Troglodyte" in *New South*; "Call It
A Hat" in *The Pinch*; "Gardenland" in *Another
Chicago Magazine*.

CONTENTS

GLOSSOLALIA

GAZELLE LEGS SPLAY OUT, *neck muscles ripple fine she dainty swig dark emerald murk at summer water hole.*

Empty belly alligator imitate vicious, hungry log, blink watchful amber eye.

Shady banyan branch. Hippo bead on both, sigh over tasty business mossy bottom lettuce.

Without half try, alligator lazy snap ragged jaws.

Gazelle, mid-swallow, caught in vise of yellow, pointy teeth.

Alligator think, "Ha! Lunch!" Saliva drool for gazelle bonbon of loin & ankle, ear & thigh.

Hippo, she say, "Fuck that shit!" Make Nijinsky leap into blood-streak whirlpool, knock alligator on the bean, pluck gazelle from slack-jaw astonish & lay her gentle on riverbank, out of daze old lizard reach.

Alligator slink down fast. Eye blast venom, appetite.

Hippo nudge gazelle sable head into her mouth, cushion fat pink tongue under skull like a pillow.

"Ha! Lunch redux!" alligator spit.

But no.

Hippo whisper secrets into blissful, ignorant gazelle. Say, "Moon is cotton & she laugh all night. Birds sing to measure the age of the world. Fish rather dance than swim. Time to run. Time to run."

Gazelle open eyes, crusty & surprise. Wishbone lungs fill with river-horse secrets, heart pound like prayer as she birth herself from hippo mouth, bow once & scamper Bambi-style away, dribbling urine like to say, "Man! Did you catch that?"

Mommy reach over shut the TV from her folding chair. "Dora, what you got to say?"

"Them Hollywood animals," I say from bed. "Went to acting school. Gonna get treats and a paycheck." Just 'cause I sick don't mean I shut up. Don't mean I can't think.

"Ain't no tricks on the National Geographical." Mommy smile because she say it wrong on purpose. She look down her lap. "Porter, what about you?"

Porter, he a big boy. Already 10, but Mommy lap he favorite seat. Still consider nature like a bible. Think a long time before respond. "Everybody know hippo vegemarian," Porter finally say, snuggle down to Mommy like he want back inside. "Wasn't never gonna eat no gazelle."

"Even more." Mommy ease Porter from between her bones. "Hippo give that little skinny the fresh minty breath of life."

Lyle Beauty come stand the doorway, rub he hands up under he shirt, show stripe hair down he belly. "You and them kids finish that TV? How you feel, Dora?" He pretend care, but everyone know "Wrestlemania" start 2 minutes. He a big child like that. Just want what he want.

"Take it," Mommy say. She flinch when Lyle Beauty yank the plug & haul the TV out the room. Her eye track down he behind way our pumpkin cat Violet sometime stare off in a corner like she waiting on a message from the wall. In looks department, Mommy definitely gazelle, especially when her eyes on fire for Lyle Beauty.

Porter put he hand on Mommy face, move it back he direction. "God tell hippo do that?" Porter ask, think maybe God is cool.

"Maybe he didn't and maybe he did. What matter hippo did it," Mommy say. "Dora, put this boy to bed." She place her mouth on he head like a pretend kiss, not the real kind with the noise so yo know you been kiss, then run out the room. "And don't forget wash his hands first."

Porter hands much littler than mine & way he look so happy when I wash them make me want to squeeze them real hard, make him cry out. But not tonight. He so full of questions about the hippo, I got to pinch him make him stop. Tuck him in tight like envelope, then go back to bed, listen Mommy & Lyle Beauty laugh they secrets while "Wrestlemania" audience cheer.

Today I get restrict to home quarantine. Grammy come over from number 9 before Mommy leave to work at Chateau de Style, where she cut & design hair. "Ain't you gone wear that mask like doctor said?" Mommy ask Grammy, dragging Porter behind her. He still mad at me for not letting him dress like a pirate for school. Pretend to be slow & sleepy zombie boy, suck he thumb & don't open he eyes he ain't got to.

"Why I need a mask for? That girl just got plain 'fluenza," Grammy say. She got her pee-yellow canary Mitch with her, fussing with seeds & making sure old Violet lock in the bathroom before she put Mitchie cage on the table.

Different kind of quiet begin Mommy shut the door. Quiet, until you listen hard. But Grammy teakettle hum. Mitch cheep like a baby chick. Violet howl & scratch the door. Bus brakes hiss a nightmare snake, maybe Anaconda. Quiet like a jungle circus.

Only thing on TV "Hogan's Heroes." Already I bore this sickly life. Slip between the velvet drape & dirty window, I secret spy on the courtyard our own Pyracantha Lysander Arms, where Lyle Beauty stand in shade behind the fluffy-prickly tree. He watch a new tenant move in. He call it supervise. Her name Miss Juniper. Lyle Beauty he know insides all Grammy 15 apartments like he own stanky underwear. Know Mr. & Miz Vazquez, number 3, got 2 sets bunk beds in that tiny 2-bedder. Know McDermotts, number 5, everything they bring shroud in blue plastic tarp & "Hog-tie like dead bodies," Lyle Beauty say at dinner. Always make me wonder how them pigs put on they ties.

Lyle Beauty tap the key ring he knee & smile. 15 keys make one hefty clank.

"What you watching, Dora?" Grammy flip a finger through the curtains & we secret agent them both. Reporting for duty, Colonel Hogan.

Miss Juniper she don't bring much except hammock & a harp. Sad eyes & bag groceries. Bottles clinking. Lyle Beauty, he wait she drag that harp upstairs, then go help put them groceries up. She give him a bottle & they talk soft 'bout hammock-style sleep. He even take extra 10 help her nail both ends, not to mention the eye-shot of pure natural breast inside the lawn-green fabric her blouse. Oh, she know it. Swing & laugh. Promise let Lyle Beauty run he callous hands her golden harp.

When Grammy rap the window, Lyle Beauty see us. He finger twitch without him mean to, like electric shock.

I know he want smoke. He ain't smoke since Mommy catch him sniff that last babysitter Nicholette. No one know, but I secret agent that, too. Lyle Beauty make me swear keep it secret or Mommy tan he hide & mine. I never say nothing, but I know Lyle scamming get some more Miss Juniper. He have ways, he think. I practically see thinky words float up over he head, all crinkly & black, fresh-type against light-brown sky. Lyle Beauty, he just tap them keys against he thigh. I hope they leave a bruise.

Crybaby sound make me & Grammy jump. "Go let that nasty creature out the bathroom," Grammy say. "Mitchie back his cage."

After lunch, me & Grammy glue macaroni to Styrofoam for Xmas ornaments. Miz Vazquez, number 3, she bring over XXL cardboard box. "Got a new refrigerator," she say. "Thought Dora, being sick and all, might like to play inside."

"New refrigerator," Grammy say. "Must be nice."

"Not really," Miz Vazquez say. "I got to have my appendix remove. My sister sent some money help with the hospital bill. Dagobert, he think we gone have just enough left over." Miz Vazquez smile my way. "You let me know you got anything you want me keep cold."

"Roger Wilco," I say. I spy with my little eye, she got scare behind her mind.

"I like to freeze old Lyle Beauty hammer," Grammy say, then she whisper something Miz Vazquez & they howl almost to tears.

Lyle Beauty make box a clubhouse in the living room, slice a window with he knife. He laugh 'cause it say THIS END UP one side the box, with a arrow point at my little face inside.

When Porter get home, he want in the club. Knock the door, make the whole house shake.

"Can't you read?" I point where I wrote PRIVATE above the door.

"No," Porter say.

"*Verboten!*" I say, like Colonel Klink. "You can't come in without the code."

"Cat puke?" Porter guess, because Violet do that right now on the carpet.

"Nuh," I say. "I was thinking 'spats.'"

"Oh, yeah, 'spats' good," he say. Porter got them brown eyes people always know what he think. Clubhouse look real fine to him. Nice safe place be inside.

"Guess again." I want him be good & jealous my clubhouse, like I'd be if he was the one sick instead me.

"Suspenders?"

I stick my tongue out. "Fur ball." Porter can't imagine I could change it every time, but I can.

"Why your tongue brown?" he ask.

Grammy say, "Take your behind outdoors, Mister Porter."

I stuck indoor clubhouse rest the day, until Mommy home Chateau de Style. "That box stink like hog heaven, Dora. It got to go outside."

Lyle Beauty take it out the courtyard. I wonder do they wear ties in hog heaven.

Still quarantine & too tired play. Think maybe I got the plague or something, feel so woozy always. Now everyone got to wear the paper mask, everyone mouth & nose wiggle up & down they talk. Look like they got a hand stuck up they throat, like sock puppets.

Grammy make me write thanky note for when Miz Vazquez get out the hospital. It say: *Dear Miz V. I hope they let you bring home your appendix. I would like to see it. Thank you for the box. It a perfect clubhouse & Porter can't come in. I hope you get well soon & me too. Dora, number 2.*

Spoil in my glory, Grammy let me lick frosting off eggbeaters & test chicken skin, check burnt crispy like everyone like. She cool washcloth my forehead & open up my hand, read my lines. "You're going to live a long and colorful life," she say, trace finger to wrist, make me squirm. It tickle good till I cough like barking dog & Grammy have to whack my back make me stop.

I secret agent Porter play outside. He know I kill him he go inside my clubhouse, so he sit next to it, like sitting near just as good. He make he hands like a bowl & stare into them, talking words nonstop. Maybe he read he own lines like Grammy do mine.

When I bore of secret agent Porter, I help Grammy clean the canary cage. "So much fun," Grammy say. "Look how happy it make Mitchie when his paper clean."

"Sure," I say, like I so sick I don't know difference between fun & birdshit. Maybe that's a result my colorful life.

"Remember," Grammy say, "funnies side up."

That's when I hear Porter laugh outside. All by himself, little creep, knocking knees together & falling over onto scraggle grass. He stare in he old hand bowl like it some kind of crystal ball, nod he head like he promise do whatever it say.

"Porter psycho," I say. "Look." Grammy join me at the window. We all use watching Porter do he things. One: He keep a bag of rocks under he pillow. Two: Every rock got a name. Three: He say he abduct by aliens. This happen mostly on Wednesdays.

Mitchie get crazy being out the cage. Try to fly at Grammy shoulder but misfire & bump my head, which scare the crap out him. "Mitchie just did it on my shoulder," I say. More colorful by the minute.

"Porter splendid boy and Mitchie splendid bird," Grammy croon, all squeaky-bird voice. Cup Mitchie in her hands, press Avon Lady lips to beak, padlock him safe back into he cage.

"They might be splendid and all, but I still feel like socking both them," I tell her.

"Go wash your face, nasty girl." She pinch my arm so I know she mean it.

When I go the bathroom, Violet spit up another pile in the corner. Puke look like a little mouse, sound asleep on cold pink tile. I fetch a towel to clean it & a small book fall out the shelf.

Dear diary, Mommy write. I skip the boring part, where Mommy dream she might like to write some day. Fixing hair nice & all & she got the knack for find people pretty side, yes, she do. But she like to tell the kind story all Mommy gonna tell every Baby & Baby gonna remember all they life. The kind story start with love & hate & end with something new. Mommy wish for drugs. Not the old kind, made her fly & wild. She want the heal kind—kind free her mind & open her soul. Kind that fillet people heart, let in the ones need forgive, the Hitlers & the Mansons. The Papa Royales. The Lyle Beauty.

I get all romantic behind my eyes. Page back where Mommy first meet Lyle Beauty. Mommy write: *I was first attracted to his mouth. It speaks to me in code. When that beautiful mouth says cigar, I know he means he wants me to rest my head between his legs and give him one fine blow job. He says it like this: see-gar. He's got a way with my sweet spot that keeps me thinking of him all day long, making it hard to concentrate from payday to payday, between cutting heads and playing Solitaire. "Casaba," he said once, pulling me out into the courtyard in the dead of night, behind the hibiscus tree, right under Mrs. Vazquez' window. I will never forget his tongue, bitter brown from coffee, his hands pulling my sweater from my skirt, the steam, Spanish radio and cutlery clattering above us.*

I remember first time I meet Lyle Beauty. Birthday party, Porter 6 year old. Lyle Beauty, he move in Pyracantha Lysander Arms number 7 that day. Porter circle he new trike in the courtyard.

Lyle Beauty stand center, like hole in a sugar donut. Chocolate pants, Pendleton shirt, hands in pockets, gold tooth whistle "Yankee Doodle." Hot spots from Grammy handheld flash glare on Lyle Beauty shiny cheeks. Already act like Papa Royale even though everybody know Porter real Papa Royale made like a banana & split.

Mommy watch Lyle Beauty watch Porter so hard her cake knife frosting splat to dirt. Hippo watch alligator watch gazelle.

He said he loved me so much he wanted to break all the bones in my arms and legs. He wanted to reset them in the shape of a perfect instrument. He wanted to spray-paint me gold, stretch catgut from my shin to my shoulder, play music on me like a symphony between love and heaven. His words made me smudged and blurry, as though I was trying to breathe something solid (earth?) through something light (feathers?). I held my breath, in case it was my last. Lord help me, I cannot resist that man.

I wonder what's blow job & promise myself: Never fall for love or man with Beauty in he name.

Wednesday morning, Mommy dress up for Chateau de Style client Felix. "Look like you doing more than Felix hair," Lyle Beauty say, all thick & spicy mean.

"How many times I gotta say Felix play the other team," Mommy snap.

After breakfast, I secret agent Lyle Beauty sniff around Miss Juniper door, fingering he hammer. He just about to swing her hammock when Porter scream from the courtyard. Everyone live in the Pyracantha Lysander Arms know that shrieky scream. It mean the aliens come again.

Lyle Beauty, he run away Miss Juniper door, go pick up Porter, pat he back. A cough come up real bad on me till Grammy give me air from the scuba diver tank.

Afternoon Mommy come home sad. Say Felix sister just die from blood-sick disease don't nobody can even say, barely the doctors. Felix say he sister weakly anyhow & ain't never been the same since they baby brother die. He write a poem & want Mommy read it since she dream of being a writer, but Mommy say no: If Felix make her cry while she cutting hair, she might chop off he ear & then they both feel bad.

"I feel bad," Porter say, but smiling like he don't know what he say.

"Why?" Mommy put down her fork.

"Aliens came today." Lining up rocks around he dinner plate, which give Grammy the crazy eyes.

"What them aliens say?"

Porter take a big swallow air, don't look at no one when he talk. "They come to kill me because I mad at Dora she sick all the time and boss the clubhouse. I wish God could kill Dora, so aliens say they gonna kill me."

Mommy say, "Not true. Can't be killing no one with wishes."

"If you could kill people with wishes, Porter be dead about thousand times," I holler. My head hurts & I want to play outside. I want to take off my clothes & roll in dirt, even though it night & getting dirty don't make no sense. I want to kill stupid Mitchie. My tongue hurt.

Mommy open her mouth, then she close it & just look sad.

Lyle Beauty look at me like he wish he could kill me, like he wish God would strike me dead or alligator come & eat me up, take awful girl away from everybody happy splashy pond. He turn to Porter. "God just make certain people mean, Porter. It ain't your fault. That girl know where she going when she die."

I hate everything. Everyone. My wishbone lungs tight from wishing I die. They gone be so sad. They be wailing about miss me every minute & what a fine child I was & smart. I'ma fly around with angels on my shoulders. I don't never need to walk, just ride the teacups instead or catch a car down the Matterhorn I want get somewhere real fast. And all the animals my best friends, even the alligator, who would chew Lyle Beauty in half with one good yellow-tooth chomp I wiggle my littlest finger.

Next night, Mr. Vazquez come over, ask can the triplets stay for supper, he got to make some arrangements. He say when the doctors dig in Lola appendix, they find cancer. They try scoop it all out, but too late. Lola she just expire. He so creep out, he can't even go the kitchen no more without see the refrigerator & think of Lola.

I never know Miz Vazquez first name Lola. Sound so close to Dora. I crumple up the thanky note my pj pocket.

Grammy make special fry chicken just because triplets company. Triplets don't say nothing. No one know which one which anyhow. They let me finish all they crispy chicken skin & flash! A sword fly through my stomach. I take a giant pill & lay down straight to bed.

Matter of fact, my funeral ain't like Disneyland at all. Ain't no stuffed animals, no teacups. I look just like myself in the pine box against the pink satin. My black hair real shiny & curled like a princess, even though the lady part the bangs on the wrong side, so when I look down at me, I look just like I use to look, only backwards, like in a mirror. & then I wonder am I backwards in the mirror or myself in the mirror & backwards in real life? I got time to think on that kind of stuff, philosophy & things I always curioused about but never got to really ponder deep because Violet always puking or Porter doing he strangeness or needing hands washed.

It just like every other day in the Pyracantha Lysander Arms, except I ain't around. First day, the fever sweep in & take me, nobody talk a whole day. After my funeral, everyone sit in the living room round the TV, except the TV not on, & everyone still looking at it, like a habit in they necks they just can't break. Porter, he been a pirate all day long. He go play my clubhouse with he bag of rocks & nobody say jack-crap.

Mommy clear her throat & blow her nose. "My piece chicken had blood in it." She say this straight to the TV, but Grammy know who she really talking at.

"Don't you blame my cooking. Dora had fine, long lines in her hands. You got to blame anyone, go blame God." She squeak back & forth in old rocking chair, hold Mitchie her hands like she praying on him & blow kissy at he beak.

"Dora sure would be fine she got a chance to grow up," Lyle Beauty say quiet, shaking change in the pocket he dress pants & looking out the window where Miss Juniper in the courtyard, smoking a cigarette & sucking on a beer bottle, sitting next to the clubhouse Porter inside.

"Don't talk like that about my baby girl," Mommy say, sharp & scissors.

Lyle Beauty swing he head around, show Mommy he surprise face. Sun in he eye make it toffee caramel, like my favorite apples. Lots words floating between them, swirling around like planets & stars, none them said out loud.

"Sometimes it don't matter who you love or how much, they die." Grammy act like she talking to Mitchie, but everybody listen anyhow. "Lotta people say people die in threes. Losing Dora one them things. Just bad Mommy luck & sorry hand lines."

Mommy stand up. Her whole body shaking like gazelle when it come out the hippo mouth. "Now Dora dead, there's no need for quarantine," Mommy tell Grammy. "I'm going to the bathroom. You be gone by the time I get back."

Grammy make her mouth like a line. Grab Mitchie in he birdcage with he shitty funny papers & head on home across the courtyard, number 9. Her door slam so loud, Lyle Beauty jump & got to pretend he meant to shake that pocket change.

"I'm gone outside for a smoke," he say, only no one left to hear it.

Mommy pull her diary from behind stack of towels. She write: *Every morning for the rest of my life, when I wake, I'll look in my coffee cup and see a bloody head emerging from my ripped vagina. I will never stop thinking about Dora. I will never stop hating God. If I were to write a story now, it would be about a soldier and a nurse, during wartime. Severed limbs hang from cypress trees like fleshy beans. I know how it feels to breathe dirt, to eat it. To nourish my belly with hate. I'll describe long lines of scarecrow men, in bandages and uniforms, shooting their best friends for a slice of moldy bread.* Mommy arm tire from all the hate come out of it, but she got more to write.

"Let Jesus carry you," Miss Juniper saying Porter. "He take care a you now your sister gone."

"You mean like aliens carry me?" Porter ask, he bare foot petting on Violet. Violet yawn & stretch, keep one eye on her boy.

"Ain't no such thing aliens." Miss Juniper suddenly Queen of All Knowledge.

"Yuh huh." Porter expert, don't care what no amateur think.

"Where they come from then?" Miss Juniper ask.

"Everyone know the sky," Porter answer. Can't believe Miss Juniper don't know that. Even Dora know that, he think. Knew.

I want tell him, duh, even babies know that, but not sure how he hear me.

"What they do when you see them?" Miss Juniper talking sexy, like Porter grown man.

"Aliens say I'm bad and deserve die," Porter explain. Pay more attention he rocks, making designs in circles & squares.

"Nobody deserve to die." Miss Juniper touch Porter shoulder. "Seven Lambs say God want us all go heaven."

"Hog heaven," I yell 'cause it feel good & I think it will make Porter laugh, but he don't hear I guess. He squirm away Miss Juniper arm like Violet do when you pet long down her back & she slink down caterpillarish, only Porter more polite. Good for him. That one got too much Jesus in her eye. Don't mean she shut up.

Now Lyle Beauty step outside the shadow the tree he been smoking under. "Porter hard to understand sometime. Stuff he say sound like he talk in tongues."

Miss Juniper look up at him like he the Sun & she bask he golden glow. "That's all right, Mr. Beauty," she say. "Perhaps he blessed. Everybody got to have something fall back on."

Lyle Beauty say, "You mean like my good looks?"

Miss Juniper smile. "That's one thing." Now she finish her bottle, she talk better, like she younger than she used to be. "Could be talent. Skill. Prayer if you like."

"How about I just say the alphabet backwards?" Lyle Beauty ask. "Or talk in code?"

"Password 'spats,'" Porter say, but nobody notice. Them two only got eyes for theyselves.

Mommy come outside now, shake her write arm like it tired & empty, shade her eye try decipher whatever going on the club-house. "What everybody doing?"

"Miss Juniper just say she play us some harp," Lyle Beauty say.

"Oh, no," her mouth say, but her eyes say, "Hell, yeah, and you better watch me."

"I don't think so," Mommy say. Her eyes match her mouth.

Miss Juniper muscle her harp down the stairs, hug her thighs round that old-school instrument. After her angel song, Lyle Beauty say, "Your hands so beautiful. I want to pound them paper-thin, bake them into pies and put them on a windowsill."

Miss Juniper so sad & thirsty, wrap in her magic music shawl, see some kind of future instead the crazy behind Lyle Beauty eye.

"Huh," Mommy huff like bull, her high-heel sandal paw the ground like to kick Miss Juniper lights out or whack Lyle Beauty on the lips. She pick up Porter, remind everybody who the rooster in who henhouse.

Miss Juniper don't know Stop from Go. She pat Porter on he head. "What about them aliens? They do anything nasty to you?" She brave now everybody know she high on Lyle Beauty list. "Make you take off your pants?" Miss Juniper whisper. "I hear you get abduct by real aliens, they leave a mark on your ass. You got proof?"

Porter, he no fool. "Fuck that shit," he say. That make me smile. I remember the day I teach him that one.

Miss Juniper sigh & look to thoughts of tongue-talk calm her down. "Proof of aliens a sign on your ass. Look, I'll show you mine." She flip up the back her plaid skirt & hike up the elastic of her pants. A large bruise laminate, all purple, green & yellow, almost big as Porter hand when he place it on her thigh.

Lyle Beauty sock him. "Don't touch, Porter."

Porter open he mouth to cry, but he don't make no sound. Just thick string snot stroll down he lip.

Mommy slap Lyle Beauty, who flash pull back he fist high at Mommy.

"*Verboten!*" I say. "Like hell you will. Step back, jack. Don't cry, McFly."

Porter eyes go wide & he look around. "Dora?" Wind pass through the fluffy-prickly tree like river rush on rocks. Blow through Miss Juniper harp like Sunday harmonica. Blow through Lyle Beauty hair like wave in pond when you throw in stones one at a time. Blow through Mommy heart like baby laugh. Everything heavy & slow.

Porter look up at Mommy with old-man knowledge eyes. "Sound like Dora happy voice," he say. "Like when Dora use sing her TV songs."

Mommy smile. She know I love themes. "What Dora happy voice say?"

"Say don't hate God. Ain't God fault she dead. She told me forgive God like you got to forgive the alligator need his lunch."

Mommy give Porter kiss, take him inside.

Lyle Beauty come home late that night, Mommy know what in he eye clear across the room. Before they start throwing yelling words, Violet hunch in front the TV & yack up something awful black & hairy.

"Violet kill something," Porter say, inspecting real close. "Plus grass."

Lyle Beauty sit down hard under Mommy glare. "It tournament night," he say. "Someone else got to clean that up."

"That's it," Mommy say. "I can't take any more suffering. Violet got to go. Mean thing probably carry fever that kill my darling Dora."

I never been call darling before. It feel nice.

Mommy wrap Mrs. Violet Deathbed in Porter old blanket. Take Mrs. V. D. to the vet emergency & say, "Go ahead. Put her down."

But the vet put on he metal vest like Lancelot. Sniff Mrs. Violet Deathbed up & down, poke her to & fro. He say, "Not this cat, lady. Not today."

Mommy take Violet home & yell at Lyle Beauty, "Why I lose my baby Dora and get stuck with this bitch?"

Next morning, Mommy won't get up.

"What I suppose do," Lyle Beauty holler. Then he disappear.

Mommy jump up from the bed to secret agent Lyle Beauty behind the velvet curtain. Watch him go Miss Juniper. Talk low & her door closing soft.

Mommy say, "Fine." Real hard. Like spit come out when she say it. "Fine."

Porter stay home, too. Dress like a pirate & chef up all the meals for him & Mommy all day long. She call him Captain Cook & Porter didn't see no aliens all day.

Mommy washing every dish because that's how many Porter use. From the whole week. Nice & slow. Hot hot water steam the windows. Spider in the corner web spin crazy around her carcass. "Grammy probably in her chair right now, waiting for me to call," Mommy tell Porter. "Old bitch wait for me to call even when

Grammy got time to call, and she know I don't because when she finally call, she say, 'It's been ten days since you call,' and I say, 'Already? I just call you,' and she say, 'Yes, that's how it feel to you ain't it? You always too busy to call,' and I say, 'So you callin' now, let's talk,' and Grammy say, 'You know what I mean,' and I say, 'So do you.'"

Porter laugh at Mommy speech.

Mommy almost smile. "Whoever invented rubber gloves, I like to marry them," she say.

Porter pour milk over Frosted Flakes & put it on the floor for Violet.

Down in number 15, jazz play so soft you can barely hear Billie, but still Miss Juniper & Lyle Beauty swinging. "What your front name?" he ask, move he kiwi fruits across her cupcakes.

"Blousie," she giggle, wave her pineapple he banana.

"I truly admire the way your head attach your neck," Lyle Beauty say, making sure the candle light up he teeth when he say it, make he words sparkle. "I want to peel back your skin with a paring knife, reveal your fine-sculpt muscle and gorgeous, blood-fill vertebrae. Excuse me. I'll be right back." Lyle belly-crawl away, run water in the kitchen. Call Mommy, number 2.

"I bet that Grammy," Mommy tell Porter when the phone ring.

"I love you so much," Lyle Beauty whisper Miss Blousie Juni-per avocado princess phone. "Your gold and your strings and your symphony."

Mommy listen background noise: radio scratch & Blousie snatch. Mommy hang up & stand quiet think. Feel like a long time before actual words appear. Actual idea. She call Grammy say good-bye, tell Porter put on he pirate suit & pack he rocks. Give Miss Blousie Juniper the fucking cat.

Mommy take Porter Greyhound. She buy ticket number 57 & leave the driving to them. Porter spread he rocks the next seat next, line up angel light vs. devil blaze. Mommy want to remind him: she hippo, Porter gazelle, but Mommy think Porter already know. He smart that way. Mommy open her diary. So many blanks she want to fill. Write: *I will go until I find a certain kind of sky. I will memorize the dappling. Recall a picnic in wind and fog, on Papa Royale's stiff car blanket, with its smell so foreign and comfortable. Remember Lyle Beauty's first kiss between my legs, the way I felt when I opened the door to pick up the newspaper and instead felt the blasting notes at a rock concert up through my seat, lost my head in clouds of smoke, and when it cleared, there were beautiful boys in open-throated flowered shirts and hip-huggers, singing and smiling down at me.*

Greyhound finally stop far out the city. Way out. Galaxies away. Air hot & dry, buildings low & old. Porter surprise. "You never told me sky so big," he say.

Mommy say, "I never knew."

Mommy & Porter walk the road. Find Sunshine Café, where a bell go off when Mommy open the door. Sunshine clouds & nature all paint up on the walls. Five empty tables & a doorway hung with strings of beads. "They diamonds?" Porter ask.

"Could be," Mommy say.

Person come out from the beads. Mommy can't say it man or woman. Got hair lady-long on one side, gentleman short the other. Face like a gate or a horse, but Mommy squint her eye to find the pretty side. Few snips here & there.

Mommy order cup of tea, peanut butter sandwich for Porter. Tea come with leaves & flowers tie up in a fancy bag. Mommy hate to wet it, but he/she/it say, "Girl, you got to live some time."

Mommy take her tea, sit in somebody old red chair out the garden. Porter watch a green & blue stripe honeybee dig holes in about 100 different places & never stop.

Mommy watch Porter watch a bee.

The End

SUPERBABY SAVES SLUGVILLE

BY THE TIME MY LITTLE BROTHER SHOWED UP, everyone was pretty much sick and tired of the whole baby thing. The Teamsters were on strike, so our dad was walking picket lines up and down the California coast instead of delivering meat to North Beach and Chinatown butcher shops in his blood-stinky van. Our mom tossed out her hospital slippers, put on black leather pumps, and hopped on a streetcar headed downtown, where her secretarial job was waiting for her to come back after she popped the little bugger out. She was happier than anything to return to the much-needed overtime and martinis with the "kids," which is what she called anyone her age without children.

Our grandmother had recently gotten divorced. She was finally living the high life, which basically meant her grand-maternal instinct rolled over and stuck all four legs straight up in the air. Instead of enjoying after-school hours in the park with her baby grandson the way she had with me, Grandma spent her afternoons hell-bent on losing the nest egg at Bingo and shopping for dresses that shot off sparks when she did the rumba or the cha-cha. Grandpa made himself rather scarce in those days, but he showed his red face every now and again to scare the crap out of us, borrow a sawbuck, and then sail away in his beautiful Checker cab number 584, which gleamed like a yellow submarine. My youthful, plentiful aunts and uncle were busy wasting time and pocket money on the so-called Summer of Love, so the chore of babysitting my brother naturally fell to me.

We spent our afternoons in Grandma's front yard. Like a jailbird, I separated rocks from dirt clods and dirt from turds in the dried-up cement square, while my brother keened for hours on end in a small wooden box in a shady corner. At first, our antics attracted a slew of visitors. The Hinterlanders, whom our uncle dubbed the Weiners, complained they couldn't hear Merv Griffin over my brother's caterwauls. The Bossanovachiks claimed rearranging the turds confused their dog Maxie (whom our uncle called Muttonhead), which gave her the runs. Bonnie J., who had just recently moved in and didn't know too much about our family, came over to introduce me to her dolly (big whoop), and brought candy for my brother, which I instantly confiscated, announcing that his allergy to sugar might be fatal.

After a few months, my brother's all-out hollering subsided to an incessant whine. The Hinterlanders turned up the TV. The Bossanovachiks switched Maxie's dog food. Cobwebs collected in my brother's ears and pigeons came to roost on him when the fog broke and the sun came through just right. It was hell cleaning their snow-white shit from his playsuit; the acid devoured the polyester nearly clear through to his skin.

About six months in, my brother got hip to the idea that the standard baby bullshit wasn't going to fly at our house, and that extraordinary measures would be required in order to get any attention. It was on toward winter now, and our pleasant hours in the rock pile had been forcibly relocated indoors. One rainy afternoon, our aunts and I were all home, watching my brother in his cage in the corner of the living room. The crying and whining had ceased; now all my brother did was sit, wobble from side to side and chew on the end of a raggedy blanky.

"Do you think he's hungry?" one aunt asked.

"Maybe he's sleepy," suggested another.

"He looks like he's gotta go," said a third.

"I think he's spying on us," said the fourth.

I was watching Merv Griffin and plucking the gold threads from the arm of Grandma's scratchy Chesterfield. I said nothing.

After watching my brother wobble became totally boring, our aunts left the room to smoke a cigarette or make a phone call to a boy or girlfriend to complain about my brother's boring behavior. When they returned, my brother was out of his cage, on his back in the middle of the floor.

"What happened?" they asked.

"Merv sang," I said, braiding the gold threads into a wristband.

"No," they said, "your brother."

He was lying on his back, raggedy blanky akimbo, glowing in a kind of stunned silence, for once not eating or shitting or sleeping or boring the crap out of us. We picked him up from the floor, returned him to his cage, then went back to ruining our lives and the furniture.

A few minutes later, we all turned around again. Presto! There he was on the floor. No one saw him do it or heard him land. Naturally, we accused each other of helping him perform this gymnastic escapade. We locked ourselves in the bathroom to prove our innocence, eyeing each other suspiciously in mirrors. When we came out, he was on the floor again, red-faced and radiant. We tossed him back in, and this time we stayed there to watch.

With the furrowed concentration of a clairvoyant, my brother closed his big eyes and curled his tiny fists. He scrunched up his face, sucked in a huge breath, then held it until his cheeks were tomatoes. With an existential moan not unlike the sound our Grandpa made while pushing a conked-out number 584 up our steep, dead-end street, my brother shivered violently, then levitated and hurled himself over the bars of his cage.

"Wow," one aunt breathed, nudging his pajama-covered foot with her toe. "He's a Superbaby."

Initially, he was. Superbaby was our shiny new toy, a plaything that delighted our craven appetites for fun. After a few days of amusing the neighbors and scaring their pets, after heated intramural debates over Freak vs. Miracle, Nature vs. Nurture, Roller Derby vs. Football, Raiders vs. 49ers, the best we could figure was

Superbaby was ticked off and he wanted some goddamn attention. This emotional craving gathered in him a kind of metaphysical strength whereby he was able to propel himself short distances. Big whoop. We grew accustomed to Superbaby holding court from the floor. Most of us even learned to step over him. We were effective ignorers. It was in our DNA.

Superbaby's next manipulation transpired in the spring, after a few brave and hearty weeds pushed their green heads through the rockpile. It was one aunt's chore to wash his rotten, stinking diapers every other day, and to add the perfect amount of bleach that would remove the crap stains, eliminate germs and give Superbaby's sensitive bottom just the right amount of irritation it deserved. Historically, Superbaby was a fantastic crapper. His habits of elimination combined Swiss-clock precision with the visceral nose punch of a Texas cattle ranch. His dirty diaper output kept our aunt's chore on a rigorous schedule, one that allowed her greasy boyfriend to hop over the fence every other day so they could make out while she tended the diapers. Like all families in our neighborhood, the washing contraption was kept in a dark shed with cracked and dusty windows, which let in just enough light to encourage the copulations of black widows and teenagers.

But on this particular washday, our aunt was surprised when Superbaby's diaper barrel was empty. No diapers, no load. No load, no washing. No washing, no making out in the shed. After five days of an empty barrel, our aunt was nose-diving toward a hormonal holocaust. It became all too apparent that Superbaby was holding it.

Like dust bunnies under a bed, we were trapped in Superbaby's master plan. We held a meeting and agreed we *had* noticed he was growing. He was now shaped like a septic tank, and our uncle used him as an ottoman to hold his TV dinner while watching the war on the nighttime news. It occurred to us that Superbaby was in danger of exploding. Action was required. We set a date for a house party and called the neighbors in to have a look. Obedient slaves we were, puppets on twine, milling around with deviled eggs and Cheese Whiz on crackers, oohing and aahing at our monument to perseverance and perversity. Mr. and Mrs. Hinterlander suggested an enema. The Bossanovachiks thought a plumber might do the trick. Superbaby lay there beaming like a Buddha, receiving boatloads of attentions from his devoted acolytes.

Grandma announced it was time for dessert, and stood at Superbaby's side with a carton of Rocky Road. We surrounded her like seagulls, clutching our bowls. Finally, Superbaby was dead center. A drum roll of flatulence sounded, and we responded to its seismic symphony instantly, nostrils a-quiver. A green cloud of noxious vapor gathered over our heads and pelted us with acid rain. We clapped our hands over our faces, but the main event was yet to come. And come Superbaby's supercrap did. A predatory masterpiece, it hissed like a python, threatening to smother us in its deadly embrace. It wound its way around our ankles until we found ourselves chained to the family members or neighbors we despised most. It snatched the Rocky Road from my grandmother's hands, slithered down the front stairs, and disappeared into a crack in the sidewalk where it seeped through the concrete into a natural spring that was incubating below our home. Once we unchained ourselves from each other, we replaced the ruined carpet, vowed never again to eat Rocky Road, and, most importantly, took turns giving Superbaby enemas if ever he deviated from his scheduled deposits by more than thirty seconds.

It was the first time we'd ever seen him smile.

Finally, summertime. It was freezing cold in San Francisco, with a fierce wind-chill factor. Over the months, the rich, primordial stew of Superbaby's supercrap had mated with our dormant spring, which bubbled up from the crack in the sidewalk and created at the bottom of our front stairs the most beautiful river of green slime we had ever seen. We loved it so much we named it. The Pississlippi rendered every foray into the world, and equally every homecoming, a harrowing adventure that threatened life and limb. Better still, thanks to the Pississlippi, what used to be a dry, wizened square of rocks and turds was now a verdant valley, a veritable Nile delta of magical mud that smelled vaguely of shit.

Mud that sucked at your feet. Mud that swallowed toys and shoes. Mud that held its shape for building castles and bridges and slabs for virgin sacrifices.

Rampant in all this beautiful mud were extended families of banana slugs. Big mustard granddaddies with foreskin hoods, shapely mothers with high-pitched, come-hither screams, horny teenagers with BB guns and cigarettes, and babies, no bigger than French fries. Although Superbaby was Slugville's inadvertent creator, under my rule, he became its archenemy. The slugs went to war against their dastardly Gulliver. They crossed oceans of mud to colonize him with their flags. They captured him, cut off his legs, dropped them into their volcano, then melted the rest of him with their flesh-eating slime. It was a marvelous summer.

Until Grandpa started to visit again. At first, he'd show up on Wednesdays, when he knew Grandma would be at the hairdresser's. His uniform reeked of cheap Tenderloin perfume, a motley fragrance of cooking oil, ladies' lingerie and WD-40. He brought consolation prizes for us all: leftover bags from Cheetah's, his daily diner haunt. The bags usually contained half of something: a cheeseburger, an order of onion rings, the infrequent grilled liver steak with real half-strips of bacon. He'd hand me the bags to disburse among the aunts and uncle, although mostly they just piled up in the crisper. Then he'd stand at the bottom of the stairs, smoking a cigarette and commenting loudly on the disgraceful condition of the Pississlippi and Slugville. "If I were still living here, I'd concrete this whole mess over," he'd propose. "Then you could play on it real nice." Grandpa always had grandiose beautification plans. At various times before the divorce, he had promised to drive a tractor through the garage to clear out Grandma's newspaper collection (it dated all the way back to the late fifties), to saw off our uncle's bedroom and put it on a raft in the Bay, and to install some nice iron bars on the windows of our aunts' rooms to keep out the boys.

This time when Grandpa pulled up, it wasn't a Wednesday at all. It was a Saturday, Grandma's birthday, and there was a party inside the house. The Hinterlanders had donated old *TV Guides* as party favors for everyone. The Bossanovachiks brought their prize poodle's puppies in a box. The Bingo team had arrived en masse, and there were even rumors of the return of deviled eggs and Rocky Road, which everyone now decided was not to blame for the supercrap incident. Superbaby and I were dressed for the occasion, with Saran Wrap bound around our Sunday shoes while we pounded out the next chapter in Slugville's violent history. In fact, Superbaby might have been overdressed. He'd had the sniffles the past month or so; now the only way he could play outdoors was in a pale blue, puffed-up snowsuit that made him look like the Michelin Man. His brown eyes bugged out like a frog's under his matching blue snow cap with the ear flaps, pom-poms and crocheted chinstrap. He was one cool Hindenburg of a customer, with the perfect innocent guise to enact his devious escape plan.

I had in my possession four prized and highly-forbidden kitchen matches, which I was going to use to light a possibly defunct sparkler left over from our July 4th extravaganza in hopes of unleashing a decent volcano on the unwary citizens of Slugville. I was packing dirty Kleenex into the volcano's crater for kindling when a dark shadow crossed the Pississlippi.

With his hands on his hips and his hat pushed back on his high, pink forehead, Grandpa was like a giant redwood tree, a forest of grandfather, looking down on me and Superbaby, squatting in the outskirts of Slugville. "How's my number-one grandson?" Grandpa picked up Superbaby and twirled him over his head.

Superbaby didn't make a sound. He was sneaky that way.

"How about a jaunt around the block?" Grandpa carried Superbaby under his arm like the Sunday paper and put him in the front seat of his Checker. Number 584 purred like a bright yellow panther; her chrome gleamed under a sudden shaft of sunlight that cracked through the foggy sky. "Fifty bucks and a jaunt around the block with my number-one grandson." Grandpa rubbed his hands together and slammed the car door so hard you could hear the eyes of all the cats and dogs on our whole block click open from their naps.

Grandpa lit up a Lucky Strike as he strolled back to Slugville. My first match had blown out in a weak whisper of wind. I cupped my hands around the second match and prayed. This was no regular old flame I desired. I wanted a flame as hot as the dickens, one whose searing heat came straight from holy hell.

"This place is disgusting." Grandpa interrupted my prayer. "What you need here is a nice lawn. For five bucks, I could roll out some sod and put up a nice swing set."

A lawn? A swing set? What did he think we were, a bunch of babies? "We already have swings on a lawn at the park," I muttered, trying not to sound ungrateful without losing my place in my prayer. If we lost Slugville, we lost everything.

It didn't matter; he wasn't listening. "How about you, Eileen?" Grandpa hollered up at the house. "You wanna go for a jaunt with me and the boy?" He twirled his cap on the index finger of his free hand.

Everyone upstairs was peeking out from behind the curtains, chewing their deviled eggs or sucking on spoons of Rocky Road to separate the marshmallows and walnuts from the ice cream. No one noticed Superbaby sitting in the cab or that number 584's motor was running.

Grandpa inhaled his cigarette all the way down to the filter, then flicked it into Slugville's tributary, where it plopped and sizzled menacingly. He swiftly forded the Pississlippi in his heavy black leather boots, leaving wet, green prints as he climbed the stairs up to the front door. Grandpa knocked the knocker till one of our aunts cracked the door, while I quickly hid the soggy butt in my coat pocket.

There was an abomination of curses as Grandpa pushed his way indoors, and the yelling started almost instantly. Even as I focused on striking the match and catching its small, bug-sized flame to a soggy corner of Kleenex, I knew that our dad and Mr. Hinterlander and Mr. Bossanovachik and probably even our uncle and the Bingo team, too, had surrounded Grandpa and pushed him back out the door, which got shut again so hard you could hear the little peephole door on the inside clang open and closed from the force. "All I need is fifty bucks," Grandpa bellowed, his lips at the peephole. "Fifty lousy bucks!"

Grandpa's face was red when he turned to face the street. He walked heavily down the stairs, making sure each footstep was loud and scary and made the wood slats creak. He stopped at the bottom stair and began to whistle, clear and loud and pitch-perfect. "Good night, Eileen. Eileen, good night." He lit a fresh cigarette, re-positioned his hat just so on his head. "I'll be damned!" he said, before lunging back up the stairs with his tree-long legs, whistling all the while. The old fart was going back in. Sure, they said no to fifty; maybe they'd be good for twenty-five, just to get him to leave. It had worked before.

As Grandpa was working up to another knock, back in number 584, Superbaby's plan was falling into place. He tried to stand up at the window to wave bye-bye, cute little sap that he was, but the puffed-up snowsuit monkeyed with his balance. His eyes got bigger as he fell backwards away from the window and onto the taxi's long bench front seat. I could barely hear his muffled laughter over the engine's lopsided rumble. Superbaby climbed back to his feet, grabbing onto the steering wheel for leverage, then continued to pull himself up by grabbing the gear stick that poked out from behind. The clunk was decisive as the engine's rumble straightened out and the car shifted into reverse.

Grandpa turned from the front door toward the street just as the taxi began to inch backwards. Superbaby was waving wildly in the window as the taxi rolled down the hill away from our house.

"Who's driving that car?" Grandpa cried out, but of course, I ignored him.

If my brother wanted to leave, I thought he jolly well should. It was no surprise to me that he would want to get the hell out. I struck another match and this one caught. I was able to light both the Kleenex and the sparkler, and I screamed as silver sparks shot out of Slugville's volcano and tiny plumes of grey smoke rose from the pink Kleenex lava. Now it was time for a rainstorm. I dumped a jar of murky, brown water into the volcano's crater. The water cut a trail through Slugville's main road, taking a couple of houses with it, as well as the fire station that had already been demolished by an earthquake caused by the spaceship landing and subsequent pillaging by the evil serial killers. The carnage was comprehensive and satisfying.

Grandpa stepped his size-fourteen boot into the middle of Slugville's main square and grabbed my arm. "I said who took your goddamn brother, and you better answer me before I take this goddamn pile of mud and dump it into the bay." He yelled it with the kind of growl that usually only came out when he was about to whale on our uncle.

"Nobody," I yelled back. "He's escaping all by himself." I pointed down the hill, past the Hinterlanders' with the ginger-bread trim that made you think a giant cuckoo was going to pop out of the front door. "And goddamn it, you're messing up Slugville!"

Grandpa turned white, as though a shade pulled down over his face. He took off running, and it was kind of funny how his expression changed when his muddy boots hit the Pississlippi and lost all traction. His tree legs flew up and his whole body became an airborne V, which was how we drew birds in art class sometimes when we were in a hurry to get to the good stuff like the wars and the battlefields and the nurses and the sex. He hit the ground hard on his bottom and out came a word I'd only seen written on a bathroom wall till then. More importantly, Slugville was safe from disaster.

Meanwhile, the taxi's big chrome grille was shrinking; it was already past the Bossanovachiks' with the gated front yard where Maxie furiously guarded the house and her puppies from intruders both real and imagined. Its back end was veering toward the middle of the street.

At the bottom of the hill at the end of the block, Mrs. J.'s big green station wagon turned the corner and was starting to climb. Probably bringing Bonnie J. home from ballet lessons so they could come to Grandma's party. Bonnie J. with the tutu who never wanted to play in Slugville. The last time she came over, she just gave her dolly the bottle to make her wet her diaper. Bonnie J. changed that dolly's underwear so much I offered to toss it into our volcano to teach it a lesson. I could see Bonnie J.'s queer-shaped head in the backseat, like a tiny Mr. Peanut. Now Mrs. J. was blowing the horn. Checker number 584 plus Superbaby had picked up alarming speed and was headed straight for Mrs. J's green station wagon.

This looked promising. I stuffed the last match in my pocket and ran yelling past Grandpa, who sat paralyzed in the Pississlippi, scratching his head in shock. I was halfway to catching up when Mrs. J. laid on the horn. I could see her big, round eyeballs and the white teeth in the back of her mouth as she hand-over-handed the giant steering wheel. The station wagon careened away from me, jumped the curb and smacked into the fire hydrant in front of Mrs. J's own house.

A geyser of brown water, which must have come from our underground lake, shot into the air and arced across the Hinterlanders' front yard. Hundreds of millions of rainbows hung in the polluted mist.

Bonnie J. leaped out of the backseat and ran over to me. I grabbed her hands and we began jumping and screaming, jumping and screaming, jumping and screaming, jumping and screaming, jumping and screaming. It was the best thing that ever happened on our block and it was all thanks to Superbaby, who had continued down the hill in number 584, which was already out of sight around a corner.

Superbaby was probably across the Golden Gate Bridge by now or on his way to Canada or Mexico or some other place where people would appreciate his amazing talent for catapulting out of cages, filling a house with a carpet of crap and popping out his brown eyes when the Michelin-snowsuit cap was tied under his third chin.

The End

TROGLODYTE

SOMETIMES I JUST KNEW THINGS. Like when the couple in the beige station wagon dropped me off at the park, I knew it was an okay place to be. They offered to buy me a hamburger and to hang out before I dove into fugitive life. It was tempting, but I was impatient to see the world with my own vision. *This is my world*, I thought, running my fingers along the manicured hedge that separated Precita Park from the street. *My world*, the expanse of lush lawn. The kiddy yard at the far end, metal swing chains clanking in the breeze of invisible riders, slide rusty at the flat bottom portion where puddles had gathered and dried over the years, monkey bars with rings on a pole. *My world, my world*, till I'd studied it all and landed back where I'd begun.

Some kids had arrived and sat cross-legged, laughing, under a tree. Maybe they were runners, too. I wanted to survive, so I thought I should mingle. I sat on a bench to devise an opening. *Hey. Hi. Hello.*

One of them came over and said, "Hey. I'm Spider. You new?" He was wrangly and his left eye blinked a lot. I didn't kid myself he was flirting.

"I guess," I said. At fourteen, I felt ancient, practically medieval. Everything around me was new, so maybe I could be new by association.

"You hungry?" Blink, blink.

Shrug, shrug, I answered, not wanting to give too much away, not so soon.

He took me over to the tree and introduced me to The Affiliation. "Like a singing group?" I asked, because what did I know?

"More like a family," Zeke said. He looked older than the others, with bits of red beard coming in along the jaw.

"But mostly like an affiliation," Sky said, pulling her shimmery gold hair into a ponytail, then letting it fall down her back. Everyone laughed except me.

Those two were the glorious ones, real movie stars who'd lived on the street a while. Then there was Princess. She wasn't what I'd call pretty, with her square thighs and tiny black eyes, but her hands were razzle-dazzle. Curiously, no one asked me my name. Maybe it was some kind of street etiquette.

Spider, Princess and I went into a grocery store on the corner. While Spider and I debated U-No versus Abba-Zaba, Princess' paws went to work, giving a thumbs-up as she left the store alone, now pregnant under her poncho. Shoplifting wasn't in the original blueprint for my new life, but I was pretty darn hungry.

We hunkered under a tree to share Hostess berry pies, beef sticks and Squirt. Afterward, we watched the weather change. Summertime here made no sense at all. The fog was unruly, shifting with the wind and the light. It whispered and moaned—or was that Zeke and Sky on the other side of the trunk?—and slid down like poured velvet over the low rooftops. Fog didn't make my head hurt like the dark clouds at home did; for that, I was overjoyed. Those were miserable days, when the sky hammocked over my head and all I could think were cheesy thoughts. Poor me, blahbiddy blah. I was still glad I'd left. So what if the chill burned through my thin T-shirt and my teeth were clacking to beat the band? Princess took pity, pulled her infamous poncho over her head, and sent it my way. It was scratchy and smelled vaguely of dog, but hers was a gleaming gesture anyhow.

When I flipped it right side out and saw the big butterfly crocheted right into the fabric, I about flew up to heaven. Last year, in
Science, I kept a caterpillar in a jam jar next to my bed. The creature went ravenous, voraciously eating for days, till it fell asleep
and became what's called a chrysalis, though it looked more like a
turd. My brother and I watched it, waiting, with him always bad-
gering and pressing against me, honking my new boobs when no
one was looking. When the chrysalis cracked open and out burst
this insect of paradise, I was so surprised my pencil went bang
into my brother's eye. He'd worn glasses since he was an infant, so
it wasn't like he was going to be an expert in the world of micro-
scopes or binoculars. I said I was sorry a gazillion times, but you
can't beg forgiveness from a belt. I took the butterfly outside so it
could live in its world. When it flitted from our fence to the bricks
then beyond, I knew it was time to quit being a turd and hitchhike
the short way to Frisco.

They sat on a bench wearing matching fuzzy, white tam-o'-
shanters. The mother cracked open a newspaper. The daughter
scampered into the sandbox. They were like Scottie dog magnets.
Watching them made my heart ache, but there was a happy side to
the ache, like when Spider asked if I was new.

I waved, to ingratiate my winning ways. The mother settled
in reading the paper, but the daughter waved back with both arms,
which was surprising, me being a stranger.

"Score!" Princess called, waving a tuna sandwich, one hand
still in the trash can. She tore it into fours and handed a section to
each member of The Affiliation.

Spider's left eye blinked. He tore his quarter in half and
handed a piece to me, keeping the crusty old corner for himself.

"Oh, I'm sorry!" Princess said, then started sexy-dancing to
music only she could hear.

"Who were you waving at?" Spider asked me.

"No one." I felt selfish: here he was giving me part of his sandwich and I didn't want to share in return. Too bad.

"Time to cruise," Zeke announced, tucking his shirt in his pants. Sky was brushing her glorious hair. They were done making out. "We do afternoons at Dolores."

"Who's Dolores?" The name sounded sad but I was instantly jealous.

"Dolores Park, man. You'll dig it." Zeke kissed Sky's cheek.

I wasn't ready to be tied down to feeling like a fifth wheel in couple world. "You go ahead. I'll see you later, okay?"

"Don't lose my poncho." Princess waggled a schoolteacher finger at me. "We'll need it for breakfast."

It was new to want something and to get it. And it wasn't like me to go and sit on a bench next to strangers. I blame the butterfly poncho.

The mother glanced up, crossed her legs, turned a page. I sat quietly, developing a crush on the mother's straw basket. It had flowers woven around the handle and an exotic, farmgirl air. I watched the kid have a love affair with the slide. Up and down, up and down. Both hands in the air, a loud, husky "Whee!" on the way down, and a mother with one eye on guard: danger and safety were an enchanting couple. Suddenly, the wind gusted and barked.

Sheets of the mother's newsprint rose up from the bench and soared over the sandbox, snapping and crackling like large, gray gulls. The kid shrieked from the slide, stretching out her arms. The mother and I jumped from the bench, chasing and snatching at the paper birds. But the wind kept laughing and teasing, puffing them just out of reach. The kid slid down to help us and we were breathless and hysterical by the time the wind quit and we retrieved all the pieces. I tried to flatten out the ones I'd caught, but they were pretty much ruined.

"Don't bother," the mother said. "No good news today and tomorrow there'll just be more of it." Her eyes were the color of the fog. She had brown, curly hair like Annette Funicello. "Thanks anyway."

"My pleasure," I said. I think I curtsied.

"Let's play," the kid said, and pulled on my hands. Her voice was deep and croaky, not the high-pitched kind most little things have. She looked just like the mom, only smaller. We amused ourselves with "Oh Mary Mack All Dressed in Black With Silver Buttons All Down Her Back" while the mother performed surgery on an orange she produced from the basket. She placed a cloth napkin on her lap, worked off the peel in a spiral, then removed the veiny threads. Even picked out the individual seeds. I myself don't mind seeds; if you make a funnel with your tongue, they spit far. But I was not about to quibble. When she reached over, pressed a section of orange into my palm and said, "I'm Linda and that's my daughter Summer," the fog cracked open, and a warm breath of sunshine poured down. I considered the venture a complete success.

The Affiliation returned shortly after the sun went down. They had scored some green off an old dude outside the church and splurged on burritos, even brought one back for me. "You're our good luck charm," Sky said.

"But I wasn't there," I said, biting into beans and rice.

"Which makes your magic even more profound." Zeke pulled at his sparse chin hairs like a professor.

Sky wedged a candle nub into an empty soda can and lit it. "For ambiance," she said, with a French accent.

"Just like camping," Spider said.

"Yeah, right," said Princess.

We sang the choruses from Top Twenty songs until the candle went out then spooned like kittens under a holey wool blanket that Spider pulled out from a hiding place in a hedge, the lawn cold and soft on our faces. The city sounded gentle at night. The whoosh of tires on damp pavement, an occasional honk. I slept with my hands jammed in the front pockets of my jeans, safeguarding my section of orange.

★   ★   ★

At dawn, our tree filled with the chatter of gossipy birds. My side ached where I'd rolled onto a root but I kept my mouth shut. Spider and Zeke had disappeared. Sky whispered and whined to her dreams. Princess was buried under a curtain of brown hair; it didn't look like she was breathing at all. I tucked my chin in my hands and observed the morning world come to life. Dads stood on street corners with lunch boxes and thermoses. Busses chuffed and groaned. Kids in uniforms with white socks and oxfords carried books, looking both ways.

I could smell my hair without pulling it in front of my nose and was beginning to annoy myself. I needed a bath, though a shower would be okay, too. I've never understood standing up to wash if you have the chance to do it sitting or lying down. My father said baths were for people who like to sit around in their own filth. I guess I didn't mind contemplating the world in my own filth, although I preferred to contemplate daily.

The boys returned with donuts and Styrofoam cups of hot chocolate. "Mmm, breakfast in bed," I said. "Thanks, Spider."

He patted me on the head and said, "Hey, no prob, chickie." His blink was starting to get to me.

As it turned out, Princess wasn't dead at all. Her head popped up and she shot me a look like, *Don't be too nice to my man.* I peeked at Spider, but he was engrossed in a jelly donut.

The Affiliation invited me to come along to Dolores, but again, I thought it best to decline. I returned to the kiddy yard. Yesterday's newspapers were still in the trash, so I dug up a piece and entertained myself with society news. Ladies with big teeth and tall hairdos like furry Russian hats smiled and dangled their sparkly earrings at men in white shirts and dark ties.It seemed glamorous to have a roman numeral after your name. I'd like to have a V after mine, like a peace sign. I was imagining my hair piled high when Summer ran up and tugged on my hand, jabbering in that surprising voice for me to play "Oh Mary Mack."

"Summer, shame on you," Linda said. "You can't treat people like that." She sat on our bench and set the flowered basket at her feet.

I decided my good deed for the day would be to broaden Summer's horizons. "Hey, no prob, chickie," I said, and led Summer into the sandbox, my platinum bouffant sparkling in the fog, my diamond earrings irradiating a laser beam light show. She made that pouty *You've got to be kidding; why are you ruining my perfect world?* face that kids sometimes make when you point them in a direction they're not used to, but in a short time she was flying, screaming for me to push harder. Once we worked out the kinks she was a natural, and I only had to push every other time to keep her at maximum height.

This time, Linda had two oranges in her basket. She taught me how to peel away the skin in a spiral and hold it just so, letting it drop gently into itself to create the illusion of a perfect orange globe.

On their way home, Linda and Summer stopped at the grocery store Princess had kyped from. I strolled parallel to them in the park, weighing the naked orange in my hands under the poncho. Linda came out with a brown bag. Summer gnawed on a meat stick. I panged for that meat stick so badly, I allowed myself a section of orange. They turned the corner on a street called Treat. Treat V could be a good last name.

I shaded my eyes from the glare of the fog, following a safe distance behind. Treat was a dead-end street. At the top a hillside of grass—an ocean of it!—waved hello. Linda and Summer went into a small cottage with brown shingles, white window frames and a front yard tall with sour grass and onion grass and lemon grass and all other kinds of wild grasses I suddenly remembered chewing when I was younger, in the eighth grade. The lights inside turned on, warm with electricity, like a bonfire in a forest. I sat on the curb with my orange. When the streetlights blinked on, I allowed myself another section, funneled my tongue and spit out the seeds. I was shaky when I slunk into the yard, but the stink of my hair pushed me on. I listened with mouse ears for danger or clues but all I heard was the far-off yipping of Chihuahuas.

Three dark, dirty windows sat at ground level below the rest of the house. I popped in another section of orange and wormed around the side opposite the front door. I beat back a blanket of spider web and pushed aside a bush blooming stickers and balls of spitbug spit. At the bottom of some stairs was a small green door with a window. It was unlocked, so I stepped inside and closed the door behind me. I stood there like an alley cat, waiting for the shape of the room to appear, enjoying the swampy basement air and the orange on my tongue, listening to Linda's and Summer's footsteps on their floor, my ceiling. I was well-versed in the ways of the dark, having spent many open-eyed nights in bed, practicing looking into it and finding things I had lost. My favorite No. 2 pencil? I found it at the back of my lucky charm shoe box by thinking about it when I couldn't go to sleep. Ditto my blue and yellow argyle sock, at the bottom of my brother's bed. I had always marveled at the size of darkness, how you could either feel completely closed in by it, like you were wrapped in a black wool blanket, or it could stick you smack in the middle of the universe, like you were a sun or an exploding star. Once my eyes got the hang of things, I could make out a pile of books on the floor. And a sleeping bag. As though they were waiting for me.

★   ★   ★

A clock radio buzzed in the morning. Linda's bedroom was directly over my head. The radio grew louder. There was thunder up there, like war drums or jungle boogie, followed by footsteps. They were dancing. I wanted to get up and dance too, but once I latched onto the hot smell of bacon and eggs and slightly burnt toast, I fell under its spell. I rolled over and pressed my face into the poncho I'd made into a pillow, and smashed my fist into my gut to quell the pangs. To distract myself, I memorized their basement, my new world. No car, which was good: no one would be coming here anytime soon. One wall was lined with old newspapers, tied and stacked up to the ceiling. Stuffing exploded from the arm of a red leather chair next to a tall bookcase crammed with books. *Ivanhoe. Pollyanna.* A familiar, throaty caterwaul came from above. Then Linda's exasperated voice: "…starving children in India." Back home, I ruled at Paralyze Tag and was able to stay frozen a long time. I waited until the front door closed, the key turned in the lock and their footsteps grew faint. They thoughtfully left the bathroom window open and positioned the dirty clothes hamper just below it.

First thing I did was use the toilet. I'd been holding it, and the pain was enormous. The bathroom was tiled in pink and green. It

42

was comfortable, the way bathrooms are. Even though I was alone, I lit some matches to burn off the stink, then set out to explore. The cottage was tiny, as though made by elves, with paneled walls and dotted lace curtains. The kitchen had a restaurant-style booth and a counter that opened into a living room with a real fireplace. There was only one bedroom; Summer's portion of it was sectioned off with a screen and had a rainbow and pink fluffy clouds painted right on the wall.

Back home, our furniture was cheap and plastic and new. Here, the coffee table was antique, posed on curvy legs and dotted with cigarette burns. An overstuffed armchair had teeth marks around one of its ankles. The big bed had a buttoned-leather headboard, scratched and marked. A Chinese-style black lacquer jewel box flourished necklaces and bracelets. The closet was bursting with dresses that smelled of oranges; I pictured Linda's foggy eyes as I pressed my face against a bouquet of sleeves. Summer's bright playclothes smelled fresh, like nature and animals. Or was that me?

The pipes shrieked when I turned off the faucet. I slid into the water and watched myself turn pink. I felt more naked than usual, as though my skin were brand-new. I ran my finger over my scar, which felt gorgeous, and I played chopsticks on it to help me relax. My first assignment was to pick a new name and try it on for size.

Autumn Treat V was much too sophisticated to pretend to be shipwrecked at sea or to mastermind hand races, right versus left, like she did in the tub when she was young. She was too glamorous to play farting submarines or to splash "The Star-Spangled Banner" with her thumbs. Autumn Treat V was the loneliest water nymph ever. She plunged under the sea to a bubble-filled underwater world, gliding through kelp, cavorting with seahorses. It was so sad and beautiful, she wanted to cry. When Autumn Treat V discovered it was impossible to cry under water, I decided Autumn wasn't a good name after all and it was time to get out of the tub.

The softness of the towels made me twinge with hunger. I tucked one around me, admiring the hush, scheming on bacon and eggs. When it came to kitchen messes I knew what was what, having slaved hours and often over a hot Shake & Bake. I was the

champ of peanut butter and apple sandwiches, and of heating up
pork and beans and brown bread from the can. I didn't mean to be
a glutton but before I knew it, I'd fried up five pieces of bacon and
scrambled the two eggs they left me. I ate like royalty—one bite of
egg to two bites of bacon and no interruptions from the peasants
at all—and grew fat and full. I found a washing machine in a little
backyard hutch and put my dirty clothes in it, then decided to put
my best foot forward. Naked as a lark under my towel, I cleaned
up the kitchen, washing all the plates and bowls and cups and
glasses and the big greasy pan—even theirs, which was no small
thing considering how much I hate to wash dishes and everyone
knows it ages your hands before their time—and stacking them
neatly on the counter.

I put my clothes in the dryer and padded from room to room,
opening cupboards, fingering papers. I knew this wasn't really my
world but being alone there was like suddenly having answers to
everything. Inside the jewel box were gold bracelets with leopard
fur, necklaces of sparkling gems, dangly bead earrings. I tried
them all on, posing like the nude statues I'd seen in art class, aim-
ing for a Michelangelo effect that didn't pan out. My clothes were
still damp, so I found a paisley dress in the closet, one that made
me look almost sixteen and busty if I pulled it tight in the back
and contorted my shoulders together.

I turned on the radio for ambiance. "Dear Kasey Kasem, This
may seem like a strange request, but I would like to dedicate this
song to my wife, Bertha. Thank you, Kasey, from Joe in Cincin-
nati, Ohio. And now, number eighty-one in Today's Top One
Hundred."

That troglodyte song came on, the one they'd been playing for
the last few weeks. I sang and boogied as the guy told the story of
going back to caveman time, and being tired of dancing alone and
grabbing a cavewoman named Bertha Butt by the hair. At the end
of the song, I flopped on the big bed and flipped off the radio. I
wanted to commemorate everything: the crack in the ceiling, the
sun through the curtains, the blue chiffon scarf draped over the
gold-edged mirror, naked with the jewelry, groovy in the dress. If
Linda took me in I could sleep on the couch. I could wash dishes

and clothes and babysit Summer so Linda could go shopping with her friends. Fantasy buzzed in my brain like a yellow jacket, making me woozy with hope, which is why I didn't worry about the footsteps on the front walk until a metal clang rang like a gunshot at the door. My whole skin electric, I bolted into the bathroom and leaped out the window. Blind with panic, I tore away from the yard and ran all the way down the hill to the park, aware of nothing but the slap of my bare feet on the cold sidewalk.

When I got to the tree, my throat was burning; I thought my chest would explode. My pits stank, something that had just started happening lately, which was really stupid and annoying and probably ruining my dear Linda's dress. I pushed deep into the hedge, found The Affiliation's stash and wrapped myself in their blanket to calm down. A few minutes later I exploded again, this time in giggly relief, when the mailman strode down the hill.

I stayed blanketed in the hedge for a while, observing the comings and goings of the park. A brown Chevy van was parked at one end, music thumping from its speakers. At the kiddy yard end, Summer was gangbusters on the baby slide. Linda stood nearby in the sand, shaking out one shoe, then another, then the other again. If sand was getting in her shoes, why didn't she just step out of the box? Why wasn't she sitting at her bench? I didn't want to think my people were mental, so I crossed my fingers and practiced some telepathy until I heard screams of laughter.

The Affiliation spilled out the back of the van, heading across the park toward my people. Spider was spinning with his eyes closed and his arms airplaned sideways. Princess had hers stuck forward, like a zombie. Sky stuck her foot out and Zeke tripped over it every time he stepped forward. Every single time. When he finally hit the dirt, Sky fell on top of him, then Spider piled on top of her, and Princess on top of them all, laughing like they'd never seen anything as funny as themselves falling to the ground. They'd stop and hold their stomachs and gasp and then start all over again. Spider beat his hands on his chest like King Kong, shouting, "Monkey bars! Come on! Let's play!" They all started hooting like chimpanzees or maybe orangutans; I suddenly couldn't remember

45

which was which. But they were running toward the kiddy yard with their hands on the ground and their rumps in the air, hooting and screaming. One minute, everyone was in their own orbit, minding their business, and the next, all the planets were about to collide. My pit stink was really flaring up now.

Summer stood at the top of the baby slide and windmilled *hello* to The Affiliation. "Watch me!" she hollered, and slid down the chute as if it were a monster roller coaster. That's when I understood why Linda was there. She was standing guard over the little nut. Protecting her from The Affiliation who were galloping toward them like beasts.

At that exact, specific moment, I wished I were older. If I were fifteen I would know how to behave when I needed to do one very small yet preposterously important thing. I let the blanket drop to the ground. "Yaaaaaaaaah," I yelled, bursting out of the bushes and heading straight for The Affiliation. My voice sounded strangulated; I was shocked by its force. It must have shocked The Affiliation too, because Princess and Sky screamed like girls and veered off in opposite directions. Zeke and Spider, who had started racing each other and were farther ahead, stopped in their tracks and loped back to check out the commotion.

They tackled me from both sides, and we hit the ground. My wind got knocked all the way out, but I didn't care. I couldn't really breathe, but I sneaked a look toward the kiddy yard. Linda and Summer were nowhere to be seen.

"Are you high?" Spider pressed his face close to mine. His Dentyne breath was spicy-sweet. "Where'd you go last night?"

My heart skipped, waiting for his blink.

"Where'd you get that dress?" Princess said, slapping my shoulder. "And where's my poncho?"

"Hey, brothers and sisters." Zeke was the dad now. "Let's not freak out."

Sky latched onto Zeke's arm and nuzzled up into his neck. "Let's go back to the van and smoke a peace pipe."

"Sure," I said. "I'll bring the poncho back tomorrow."

Princess scowled. I followed them to the brown van, though I couldn't have cared less about smoking a bogus peace pipe. I was relieved the universe was intact and hoped Linda hadn't recognized her dress.

Music was still blasting from inside the van when we got there, and Zeke had to knock twice on the back door—really pound it. The door opener was older, in his twenties. He wore a red knit cap and round, mirrored glasses. His black hair bushed out at the sides and his gnarly beard grazed his chest. I had never seen so much hair on a man. "If this van's rockin', don't bother knockin'," Blackbeard growled, and started to pull the door closed again.

Zeke stopped the door with his hand. "Come on, man. My kids need a peace pipe."

The van's inside walls were covered in posters that glowed under a little black light. I had never smoked dope before. Zeke promised it would make everything float but instead my brain closed over. The dark clouds of home rushed in like a riptide. I felt dizzy and sick. "Quick, she's going to blow!" Spider and Zeke picked me up and helped me outside. I heaved into the gutter, too tired to be embarrassed. There wasn't all that much to heave. When I woke up, it was dark. I was in the hedge, under the blanket. The Affiliation and the brown van were gone.

As I ran leaping from shadow to shadow, I knew it was peculiar that home meant the cottage at the top of the hill. I blame my big, pounding heart for making me slam the basement door as though it was my old bedroom door. For making me forget I was supposed to be incognito. As soon as I stepped into the dark, everything above me that was normal suddenly became very not.

"Who's there?" Linda called in a scaredy-cat voice.

I almost answered and slapped my hand over my own mouth to shut up.

"Mommy, do we have a ghost?" The reedy voice of Summer.

"Don't be silly," Linda said. "It's just a lost kitty." Then footsteps and the front door opening.

I squeezed myself behind the red chair with the popped-out stuffing and shut my eyes. I knew that didn't mean I was invisible or anything, the way I used to think when I was young, but it made me feel better. The way hiding in the upstairs hall closet made me feel safe. It smelled Lysol-clean in there and before I got too big to fit, I could squeeze in behind the stack of soft towels. Close my eyes. Drift away.

The basement door opened. I held my breath, my heart pounding in my ears worse than a parade of drums. I remembered reading about the perils of Anne Frank and was sorry for her all over again.

"Here, kitty, kitty," Linda called. A flashlight beam swirled around the room. "Come out, come out, you naughty little cat."

How badly I wanted to see her, to look into Linda's brave eyes. To follow the curl of her hair. I waited a long time after she left before crawling out from my spot. I would have to be a much more careful and quiet ghost. I lay back on Sky's poncho on the old sleeping bag and smoothed my hands down the front of Linda's paisley dress, now dirty and torn. I wondered if anyone missed me, my mother with her premonitions, my father with his backhand. Or my brother, now that my boobs weren't around for the honking. No doubt he was wallowing in the glory of my absence, stuffing his face with the chocolate pudding I made before I left. If nobody missed me, then who was I? I slid a book from the shelf and blew dust off the top. The leaves were dingy and yellowed, but in the back were stiff, glossy pages with black-and-white photos. Pollyanna was a teacher's pet kind of girl, with queer, waist-length ringlets and plain librarian clothes. Her smudged, dark eyes made her look old and seductive. I stayed up all night and read the whole book.

★   ★   ★

I was climbing a white ladder that went straight from the ocean to the clouds when the creak of the front door woke me up. I struggled to stay asleep. I didn't want to lose the feeling of climbing the ladder knowing that something truly magnificent was at the top. Something better than I don't know what: unicorns or egg salad sandwiches or a sectioned-off corner of a room behind a screen painted with rainbows and clouds. But I didn't have time to figure it out. I had eaten three of those mini white-powdered donuts, fallen asleep in the tub, and now there were intruders. I snatched Linda's dress from the floor and jammed out the window.

"Put this under your tongue and then we'll tuck you into bed," I heard Linda say. "Did you leave your dirty bathwater in the tub?"

"I didn't take a bath today." Summer's kazoo voice echoed against the tiles. My tub water glugged down the drain. "If there's a kitten, can we keep it? Please?"

"Maybe," said Linda. "If there's a kitty."

I had never been outside with no clothes on before. I felt like a giant baby. I was the Pink Panther from the waist down, because I loved to make the water as hot as it would go. When the toilet flushed, I tiptoed around back to the laundry hutch.

I buried her dress at the bottom of the pink plastic laundry basket and that's when I discovered the real bonanza. A white sweater so soft it could have been made from exotic rabbits, wafting her unique perfume. There was a small yellow stain on the front of the left thigh of white jeans. I imagined Linda drinking champagne with a prince or a baron, laughing over a private joke about snowflakes, his hand knocking her glass as he brushed tousled hair from her eyes. With safety pins at the waist and the long legs cuffed up, her jeans fit me perfectly; I felt like an angel or a cloud. I wished I had eaten more of those donuts, but I couldn't bear to leave Linda and Summer. I slipped back into the basement and listened to The Sound of Music with them through the ceiling. By the time "Edelweiss" came on I was more than halfway back to that white ladder feeling.

There was a man in our cottage. I knew because when the sound of the doorbell woke me up, it wasn't a *ding-dong, Avon calling* sound. The person who rang it had a heavier hand, attached to a bulkier footstep with a wider space between steps. The floor vibrated differently and so did the joists and the beams over my head; their boards creaked, not used to his weight. I heard him try to make Summer laugh. The old nickel behind the ear trick, no doubt. She wasn't having any of it. She fussed and whined and gibbered baby-talk, while Linda apologized and admonished, administrating tuna casserole. I wondered what he was doing up there but it didn't take long to find out. Summer went to bed right after dinner. Probably still tasting raspberry Jell-O on her dark-red tongue.

I was getting so worked up and hungry thinking about tuna casserole and Jell-O that I didn't notice the radio music playing above me or the little shuffling steps or Linda's muffled laughter. It was the "Troglodyte" song again. Linda and the man thumped their feet wildly. A little too wildly, because I heard her call out something like "Jazz!" before the scream. Then there was a scraping sound, maybe wood against linoleum. But it could have been wood against bone or hand against backside or fist against head or shoe against shoulder. All these possibilities made me crazy, and maybe I cried, "Stop!" Or maybe I kicked the red chair, I can't really recall, but the next thing I knew, Linda and Jazz were outside my basement door window.

They were in profile by flashlight, just like those cameo ovals above the TV at my old house. I timed my roll behind the red chair while they were opening the door. The light flashed in circles, like Hollywood searchlights, but it sure didn't feel like the Academy Awards. Mostly, I tried not to think about spiders or mice or to jinx myself into sneezing from the cloud of dust my rolling kicked up.

"That sleeping bag always been there?" Jazz asked. I wanted to hate his voice but I couldn't. It was just a regular TV commercial voice, with no accent. A voice that sold things.

"I don't know," Linda answered, all girlish and concerned. "I never really poked around down here before. I don't like to go to dark places alone."

"Honey, that's just an open invitation to trouble."

An open invitation? I clamped my hand over my mouth to keep from shouting.

"Don't you worry," he went on. "We'll get rid of your ghost." The zipper pull tinkled as Jazz threw my sleeping bag over his arm. "Like you said, it's probably just a cat."

★   ★   ★

I was so worried about making noise and instigating another research expedition, I hardly slept that night. I must have stayed curled in a tight ball the whole time, because when I finally woke up, my legs were still sleeping and prickly. I didn't look much like an angel or a cloud when I crawled out from behind that chair. I was starving out of my skull. I listened hard for a while to make sure the upstairs was empty, even though I knew it was far later than I'd ever slept before.

It was so peculiar when the little green door wouldn't open. I kept turning the knob this way and the other; it didn't catch and open the way it always had before. My brain refused the reality, and I kept making up possible/impossible excuses for the door not opening. It had swelled during the night. The house had shrunk. I was still asleep, dreaming the door wouldn't open. Something was wrong with my hands.

I was a much better athlete in P.E. than evidenced by my window-breaking arm that morning. I would have broken the window perfectly if Pollyanna hadn't been so heavy and I wasn't so hungry. I didn't see the blood or the jagged flap of skin until I was outside. Who knows how long I stood in the front yard. I was mesmerized, hypnotized, transmogrified by the color of my blood. How could little old me—skinny and scabby, dressed in filthy clothes that weren't mine and didn't fit—be filled with such a beautiful, rich color? And the blood ran like water, too. I always thought it would be more lazy, like maple syrup. It was so amazing I wanted to cry.

But I didn't. I held my dripping arm away from me and walked to the park. I found a sheet of binder paper with a spelling test on it (I tried not to be too hard on Nancy; "renaissance" wasn't an easy word) and wrapped it around my arm, then scrounged up a brown bag with the rest of somebody's lunch inside. A bunch of grapes and half a salami sandwich, both of which I ate too fast, making my stomach ache. I tried to see what time it was by the sky but the fog was so high and bright I couldn't even pinpoint the sun. I tried remembering *The Sound of Music* songs to make me feel better, but "crisp apple strudels" and "schnitzel with noodles" made me hungrier, which was the opposite of the point.

The brown van was parked in its usual place. The driver's seat was empty but the vehicle shook on its wheels. Voices rose from the back. Suddenly the rear doors banged open and The Affiliation flew out. Spider first, his blue work shirt unbuttoned and flapping like a superhero cape in slow motion, followed by Sky, ethereal and weightless as usual, then Zeke and finally Princess, who was topless and crying. Her feet scarcely touched ground when Blackbeard hopped out, slammed the back doors and bounded into the driver's seat. The van sped away, tires squealing. Princess's red face was twisted. Weird animal sounds came from her mouth. Her boobs were slouchy and loose. She was no longer just a girl but a woman. I wished I had her poncho so I could give it to her right then but I felt so far away. Like I was watching them on the five o'clock news instead of right in front of me.

"Come," said a voice at my elbow.

Linda was standing there, her straw basket over her arm and one hand over Summer's eyes. She grabbed my clean hand and turned me away from the scene.

I wanted to look back over my shoulder, to see Spider removing his shirt and wrapping it around Princess, blinking only for her. To see that Princess had quieted down and Sky was shushing and kissing her, smoothing her hair. But I couldn't look. Didn't glance. Didn't try. I didn't want to be disappointed. I didn't want Linda to let go.

We were walking so fast, the only thing I could concentrate on was that straw basket with the plastic flowers. It reminded me of Little Red Riding Hood and by the time I remembered the whole story, Linda had taken me into the grocery store and marched all the way past the section where Princess kyped the Squirt and the pies, right through a curtain of tinkling beads, and into a dark storeroom. Summer waited at the doorway while Linda guided me past crates of lettuce and carrots, past shelves stacked with canned goods and sacks of flour and sugar, salt and potatoes. We went into a tiny, pale yellow bathroom lit by a bare bulb. She put down the lid and pointed for me to sit. There was nothing for me to do but obey.

She peeled the spelling quiz off my arm, made a good lather with a rough bar of grimy soap, then carefully washed me. "Those are my clothes, aren't they?" she asked softly.

I couldn't bear to look down at the beautiful white pants I'd ruined with my blood, so I nodded and stared up at the most successful no-pest strip I'd ever seen in life, thick with the bodies of flies.

"I got that sweater on sale for five dollars," she said as she swabbed my gash with alcohol. "It looks real good on you. Your skin tone is perfect for white."

She went on talking about fashion and things. I couldn't concentrate on what she was saying but I didn't want her to stop; her voice gave me rubber tree plants in my belly. When she finished wrapping my hand in cotton, she asked me my name and I told her.

"Well, Coco," she said. "I would be most honored if you would accept my humble invitation to dine *chez nous* with us tonight. Now, what is your favorite meal?"

It was totally bizarre to find myself back in my bathtub. The white pants and the sweater had disappeared. Linda told me to keep my messed-up hand out of the tub so the dressing wouldn't get wet; hand races were out of the question. I didn't much feel like playing farting anthems or sea nymph. I didn't want to think or remember or plan or pretend. I just wanted to feel clean.

After I toweled off, Linda gave me a pair of blue capris and a yellow sweater. I wanted to tell her how their colors reminded me of the day when I danced in her room. The blue scarf on the mirror, the sunshine through the lace. She pointed me toward the living room with Summer, who begged for *The Sound of Music* again. Only then did I allow myself to conjecture they might let me stay. Or adopt me. I could become the nanny. Or maybe a nun.

"Coco!" Linda called from kitchen. "Time for dinner! Coco?"

I'd almost forgotten who I was.

She sat across from me in the little restaurant-style booth. I thanked her and tried to look into her eyes but she looked away. The meat loaf was delicious, with rivers of ketchup on top and canned French-fried onions on the side. Plus au gratin potatoes with orange cheese burned just how I like. The green beans squeaked merrily against my teeth when I chewed; the pound cake with Cool Whip was heaven. Everything was so delicious, I knew leaving home was the right thing to do.

"This is my world," I told them, when Officer Kelly arrived to take me away. "This is my world."

The End

CALL IT A HAT

DMITRI SHOSTAKOVICH – Concerto in C minor for Piano, Trumpet, and Strings, Op. 35. Orchestration: solo piano, solo trumpet, and strings.

Igor Stravinsky – The Rite of Spring. *Orchestration: piccolo, 3 flutes, alto flute, 4 oboes, English horn, 3 clarinets, E-flat clarinet, bass clarinet, 4 bassoons...*

Lydia tried to concentrate on the program notes, but couldn't keep from glancing at her wristwatch. Three minutes past eight. The orchestra was seated, the instruments tuned, the conductor had yet to appear. Ushers continued seating latecomers. Lydia's heart pounded; the nape of her neck dampened behind the collar of her creamy, special-occasion blouse. She fought the urge to recross her legs, and forced herself to remain still. Just a bit longer, and second-row, center was hers for the night.

In the Concerto for Piano, Trumpet and Strings, Shostakovich combines humor and introspection side by side. Sudden shifts from one temperament to another juxtapose the naïve with the complex, and humor with sorrow.

"Excuse me." A gentleman tapped her knee. "I believe you're in my seat."

"I am?" she drawled softly, feigning surprise. It was acceptable practice at the symphony for cheap-seaters to migrate forward to fill vacant seats after Intermission, by which time it was assumed the rightful ticket holders wouldn't arrive. But Lydia loved to be up close to the music and hated to wait. She had become expert at occupying the empties at the beginning of the performance and had never been questioned before. "Are you sure?" She looked up slowly and smiled, hoping the diversion would grant her some time.

"No harm." His espresso eyes were shot through with amber shards and smiled back in a way that made Lydia suspect he knew her secret. He had a high forehead, sandy hair, full lips and slightly protruding ears. Like Stravinsky, Lydia thought, and bit her lip to keep from smiling. The crystals that dripped from the wall sconce behind the gentleman shot prisms of light around his head. "I'll just sit here." He settled into the adjacent vacant seat. "It's about to begin."

Lydia returned to her program, a flush deepening in her cheeks. She dried her moist palms on the velour seat cushion.

The gentleman set his elbow (forest-green herringbone, suede patch) on the armrest, unleashing the scent of apples and bed-sheets, and there it remained when Lydia innocently raised her hand to turn the page and flicked her finger against his hand. He didn't start, didn't look, didn't even acknowledge the contact. She wondered whether to retreat, thereby surrendering the armrest for the duration of the performance, or whether to hold her ground and battle out the boundary during the first movement, when a second masculine voice interrupted.

"Excuse me," this one said, standing just beyond Lydia's neighbor and addressing them both. "But you're in our seats."

"Are we?" Lydia's neighbor asked.

"We've had the same ones for twenty years!" the man snapped, emphatically waving two tickets.

"Looks like we're busted," Lydia's neighbor said. He helped her to her feet, took her arm, and by the time they crab-walked out from the center of the row and stood at the aisle to scout for two vacant seats, the lights had dimmed and an usher appeared to escort them from the auditorium.

Stricken, Lydia followed the gentleman into the deserted lounge, where she found herself inexplicably holding his hand.

"Exiled from Shostakovich," he sighed. "May I buy you a drink? Champagne?" Lydia nodded mutely, watching their reflections in the large plate glass windows, through which she could see the plaza, with its trees wrapped in sparkly lights, and towers of water shooting up from a fountain. He returned and raised his flute. "Maybe we can sneak back in after intermission. Those front rows are fine, aren't they?"

"I know the players' footwear by heart," Lydia said.

"To the *Concerto in C minor*," he said.

She clicked her glass to his. "To *The Rite of Spring*." Lydia drank, then cocked her head to listen to the muffled music from behind the paneled walls.

"Hmmm." He nodded and closed his eyes, listening, too.

When the piano's leisurely movement ended, she finally spoke. "My name is Lydia."

"Franklin."

They gravitated toward the bar for a second round, neither of them having much else to say. When the bartender, in an effort to kickstart their conversation, confessed he was an undertaker during the day and had once built a custom casket to house both a motorcycle enthusiast and his Harley, Lydia and Franklin laughed and quickly moved on to childhoods, books and a surprisingly lovely session in bed.

A year later, Lydia and Franklin had successfully merged their lives to include one address, a wall of books, a tasteful CD collection and Johann, a goldfish Franklin had bought Lydia "just because." By fortuitous coincidence, the philharmonic was performing the same program he and Lydia had missed the night they first met. To celebrate the anniversary of their meeting, Franklin purchased second-row balcony tickets and supper at a tony downtown grill that specialized in tiny, exquisite portions for the pre-concert crowd.

Franklin was garrulous over dinner, engaging the wine steward in conversation in a mixture of Italian and French, planning idyllic vineyard vacations that hinted suspiciously of honeymoons, asking whether Lydia preferred summer to spring, if she had ever crashed a symphony hall in Vienna, proclaiming her collarbones luscious, then gazing at her meaningfully over forkfuls of chicken Marsala.

Behind the collar of a new taupe satin blouse, Lydia's nape grew feverish. Was Franklin going to ask her to marry him? Was this the moment? Was this "It"? They shared a chocolate crème brûlée for dessert, during which a staticky recording of a tin-pan piano and a jazzy blues singer begging "do me like you do" purred from the speakers. The queer song suddenly reminded Lydia of Lester. He was the one before Franklin, the one who made Lydia feel invisible by day and uninhibited at night. Lester held no promise for the future nor did he ever pretend to. Even after eight months, he wouldn't let Lydia call him her boyfriend, wouldn't even show her his apartment.

When Lydia called Lester shortly after meeting Franklin to tell him their nighttime flings were history, he asked her to go out with him one last time. She impetuously agreed, then phoned Franklin to tell him she couldn't attend his mother's birthday party that night due to a migraine. As soon as she hung up, she ran out the door to meet Lester, without even stopping to brush her teeth or splash between her legs.

Once at the Prestige Inn, Lydia and Lester fell into bed without preamble. She was twelve, she was twenty; she was bad, she was good; she was shy, she was nasty; she was sweet, she was mean. It didn't matter how she was—Lester fucked her with no distracting murmurs of love or charm. She left exhausted the next morning and threw herself into bed to soak up the last bit of fucking Lester before she had to dress to go to the movies with Franklin that night. Dear Franklin, who was so thoughtful, had left a message enquiring about her migraine before assuming she could keep their date.

Lydia had not heard from or even thought of Lester again, until that singer sang "do me like you do," Because of it, all Lydia could think of was the way Lester rubbed his face red between her legs until she cried. But she didn't miss Lester. Of course not! Not when falling in love with Franklin was so easy. Easy and pleasant. Franklin was kind, dependable, spoke bits of French and Italian, included Lydia in all aspects of his life, found her collarbones luscious and, like Lydia, enjoyed the occasional breech in the social contract.

"Nice song," Franklin said, and impetuously bought the CD on the way out to play in the car on the way to the philharmonic, which was now housed in a sumptuous new space with stainless steel curves that made the building seem like a galleon prepared to set sail. By the time they were riding the escalator up to the lobby from the bowels of the parking structure, "do me like you do" was seared onto Lydia's brain, and her mood had progressed from a loathsome nostalgia for Lester to annoyed loathing for Franklin. What if he did propose? Could she say "yes" to a lifetime of pleasant and easy spiked with obsessive recollections of "do me like you do?"

They reached the lounge on the terrace, where Franklin went to buy cordials. Lydia looked out across the steel and glass atrium and shivered. She turned to see if Franklin had remembered to bring his gloves, and thought she saw him smiling at someone across the room, but when she looked to see whom, she saw only a woman in a red dress. The sort of woman Franklin wouldn't look at twice—wearing makeup that tried too hard—in a style of dress Franklin wouldn't care for: tight-fitting, flashing with rhinestones.

"Who was that?" Lydia asked when he returned.

"Who, darling?" he said, placing his hand on her waist. "Mmm, you're turning me on," he whispered close to her ear.

"No one." Lydia felt sad for the woman in the red dress, who chewed gum with her mouth open, swung her pocketbook a bit too wildly, and placed her hand over her mouth to stifle a belch that offended no one. A year ago, it had been Lydia standing alone before the performance, trying to savor the Kir Royale she desperately wanted to slug down; attempting to appear at ease in her solitary excursion. Lester would never have accompanied her nor would she have wished him to.

The last bells chimed. Franklin took Lydia's plastic cup and tossed it into the trash. They walked to a side door marked "Orchestra," where a red-jacketed usher held up a gloved hand. "Tickets, please."

"Oh, we just want to go in for a look," Franklin said smoothly, waving his tickets in the absent-minded professorish way Lydia found so beguiling.

"Sorry, sir. You can look all you want," the usher said, staring him down behind thick-lensed spectacles. "After the show." She appropriated his tickets and brought them close to, then far away from her eyes. "You're up at the top, sir. In the back. Let me escort you. The show is about to begin, and there's no late seating."

The usher led them up three flights of winding stairs covered in garish, floral wall-to-wall, then down a crooked hallway lined with glass. When they emerged from an ill-lit, oddly-angled passage and found themselves eye-level with the wooden ribcage of the auditorium's light scaffolding, Lydia felt like she had entered Alice's rabbit hole. She leaned over the rail to peer down onto the orchestra far below, nearly swooned and fell back on her heels.

"We're in the belly of the whale," she said, and laughed to disguise the stars that swam in her eyes.

"It's all this Douglas fir. Makes you feel like you're inside a cello," Franklin said. "Will you look there?" He pointed down to the second row on the main floor, at two empty seats toward the center. "Waiting for us." He touched Lydia's hip to guide her down the steep stairwell. "We'll try again at Intermission," he whispered, then directed her to their row.

Focus, Lydia told herself. She located a point in the near distance and made it her guiding light to prevent her from toppling absurdly over the thin, burnished aluminum side rail into the open-lidded grand piano. Imagine the horror of that! A swan-like, headfirst dive, with Lydia's meadow-colored skirt fluttering at her ankles until she hit the strings with a cacophonic screech, landed with the skirt flopped over her shoulders, and revealed to the audience that on the first anniversary of the most successful relationship she had ever been party to in her life, she had defiantly donned the most pathetic piece of underwear in the drawer— frayed and saggy, with shredded elastic. Lydia worried the panties signaled an underground act of rebellion. Did she unconsciously wish to undo her future with Franklin? And even so, hadn't the hints he dropped at dinner blasted that desire for the uprising into general disarray? What did she have against paradise anyway?

"Almost there," Franklin announced. "Seats thirty-nine and forty-one."

Lydia maintained course, grateful for the serene beacon, the lighthouse, which distracted her from the whirl of color, babble of conversations, honk-and-blurt of instruments and intersecting planes of the walls around her that conjoined to create a precocious visual and aural screech. So determined was Lydia to stave off vertigo, it wasn't until she arrived at her assigned seat that she realized her lighthouse was not just a lighthouse: it was the toupee of the man in front of her.

And not just any toupee. This toupee seemed to have been fashioned from matted, bloodless roadkill. It was a dreadlock skullcap, a welcome mat of frizz. A hideous, frightful concoction that perched on its owner's head as though it owned him, not bothering to cover his hairless pate past the tops of his catcher's mitt ears, and leaving the eggshell skin on the back of his head naked and raw as a baby bird's.

The toupee's owner turned and looked up at Lydia. She abruptly cut her eyes away to a place just above it. To safer, higher ground. Make no mistake, this new spot promised. Lydia is not looking at your head. Or your hair. Whatever you call it. Your hat. Lydia is looking at me, this spot just above it. In fact, Lydia is so very much not noticing you or your hair, she's going to look you straight in the eye.

When she did, she saw eyes that sparkled like lasers in the shadowy lamps of the hall. Eyes that burned, flickered and smoked. Blue lights in velvet darkness, illuminating the way for stealth jets of insight. Eyes with a manic stillness that saw too much. Of everything. Pain. Wasted paper. The extravagance of ideas that went nowhere. Slings and jeers, imagined or real; it made no difference, they were seen and felt.

Lydia hovered halfway between standing and sitting, grimacing a smile. *I acknowledge you,* the smile relayed, *but not your extravagant hairpiece. I may sit just behind you, but our worlds orbit furiously in*

*opposite directions. Our ticket numbers are identical save for one letter, but we
have nothing in common, nothing.*

Franklin was already seated. "Comfortable?" he asked, opening his program to find the length of the pieces, calculating his
intermission hustle to the men's room and bar.

"Perfect," Lydia said. She sat and pulled her embroidered
blazer about her shoulders. As she bent to stow her matching bag
beneath her seat, she quietly breathed in her neighbor. He had
no smell. None at all. He was neutral, as though he had no effect
whatsoever on his surroundings, made no ripple in the pond.

Good, Lydia thought. I won't have to worry about sneezing.
She settled back into her seat. The lights dimmed and the Shostakovich Concerto in C minor for Piano, Trumpet and Strings, Op.
35 began. Lydia closed her eyes and slipped away on the opening
flourish for trumpet and piano, then down into the broader, darker
themes underscored by the strings and the solo trumpet's solemn,
sustained notes.

His name was probably something like Alistair. He would
speak softly. With a lisp. Perhaps an accent. Definitely orthodontic
scaffolding hooked into pink gums, guarding soft palate, nudging
crooked teeth into place. There was a general disregard for hygiene,
which Lydia fact-checked in the smattering of dandruff across the
shiny shoulders of last decade's gabardine. If she were to nudge
his shoulder with her pump, he would turn around and apologize,
and when they engaged in that full-on eye contact, she knew she
would be locked into his gaze. If Alistair spoke, she would have no
choice but to listen, for beneath the unfortunate skullcap no doubt
was a razor-sharp intellect. She would be kind, witty; she would
be free to flirt. He would be thankful for her attention; she would
be beholden to his gratitude. Beneath his rayon and worn cotton
vest beat a generous, true heart; a soul milled with passion and
flair. The knowledge that she was one of the few who knew this
would embolden her to laugh and (somehow, in her fantasy) place
her hand on his thigh, which would be surprisingly hard from
all the miles of walking he did, miles alone, and there would be a
sharp intake of breath on both sides. A meaningful, long-lasting
relationship was certain, for she would never be able to tear her

gaze from his eyes, whose manic calm she now saw more clearly as the sparkling of a child or the knowing, impenetrable bead of a crow, and she was no longer ashamed of his mangled toupee. She would just call it a hat. Yes, a hat, and it was merely another part of him that she loved and indulged, like his penchant for radishes and glen-plaid vests, or his habits of rising to pee in the middle of the night and forgetting to buy new socks.

Lydia was wondering if Alistair wore his toupee during sex, when the first movement abruptly ended. She coughed discreetly along with the rest of the audience, who had been saving up throaty ejaculations since its beginning. Franklin offered Lydia a tissue and a lozenge, but she waved them away. When she realized she might have seemed annoyed, she grabbed Franklin's hand and pressed his knuckles to her lips, inserting the tip of her tongue between two fingers. He smiled mischievously at her and winked as the elegant moderato began its brief, rich interlude.

Its simple eloquence made Lydia feel violently modern; she peeked to see if Alistair had noticed their wanton public display. Franklin was her treasure, Lydia knew this in her heart. Yet, as the violins swelled anew, tears sprang to her eyes, and her chest tightened with a suppressed sob. For how did she repay Franklin for his kindness and devotion?

First, she removed Alistair's clothes. He would want her to pair his mismatched socks and hang up the pants that didn't suit his jacket before she climbed onto him. She would refuse. Maybe even reprimand him for making such a request. Alistair's hands were soft, like a woman's, and she tied them to the bedposts with the long, silky scarves she reserved for chamber orchestra events. Alistair seemed frightened. And why not? What woman had ever captured him the way Lydia had? She reassured him with her eyes that he was in no danger, but no words issued from her mouth as she brought her lips to his muscular thighs.

Alistair moaned and writhed in response, his head twisting from side to side beneath the resolutely stationary toupee. Why won't he take it off when we make love? Lydia wondered. Didn't he know she would love him without it? What if she were to become obsessed with what was under there, or where it came from,

63

and why? When she gently prodded him for information, Alistair would tease her at first.

"Who wants to know?" He'd smile over the rim of a chipped teacup and offer a basket of scones.

So she would stop asking, because she loved him, she loved scones, and if everything else was right in their world, there was no need to delve. But someday, maybe following an argument or a night of bad sleep or an unfortunate dream of broken teeth, the question would crop up again. And after a while, Alistair would stop offering scones and become close-lipped and tight about his toupee, until one day Lydia would realize he was back in his own universe, he had let go of her gaze, had shaken her off. And she wouldn't even care anymore, because she could no longer see the gleam of his eyes in the shadow of his snaggletooth and the smell of the radish breath, and it would be all she could do not to suggest Head & Shoulders, and they would sadly shake hands and say goodbye. There'd be no fighting or bickering or name-calling or therapy, and Lydia would be sad but enlightened as she walked away and wondered why she couldn't just be happy the way she knew how to be back when she was able just to call it a hat.

Franklin's program crackled. Lydia watched him turn the page ever so slowly, in order to make the least possible noise, a practice which Lydia felt actually compounded the annoyance factor, a theory she and Franklin had once debated so hotly that Lydia accidentally closed the car door on her hand and dissolved into tears in the parking structure, and Franklin put her fingers in his mouth to make them feel better.

The moderato drove into the final movement, fraught with madcap chases, a brilliant Spanish-sounding trumpet, and delicate pizzicato strings that buzzed under Lydia's skin like bees in a hive. Franklin was still turning the goddamn page.

Lydia snatched his program, snapped the page shut and slapped the book in Franklin's lap. A giggle burst from Franklin's throat. The row of heads immediately before them jerked and shushed in disapproval.

As soon as the clapping ended, Franklin rushed away to the men's room. Lydia followed leisurely. She would go to the ladies' room and then meet him at their prearranged spot. She flushed the toilet and wondered how couples managed to stay together for years and years; not only how but why? As she was washing her hands, Lydia noticed the sparkling red dress in the mirror over the basin next to her.

The woman caught Lydia's eye and smiled. Her top teeth protruded over her bottom lip in a way that was half beautiful and half beaver. Lydia smiled back, and watched from the corner of her eye as the woman applied bright red lipstick over those big, soft lips, which pressed together, then opened in a smile, revealing the terrible, amazing teeth.

"I saw you before with Franklin," Lydia imagined the too-red lips forming the words. "Does he still swing? Does he still take those crazy photographs?" The prospect was so thrilling and confusing, that Lydia found herself attempting to rinse soap from her hands three inches above the spigot. When she finally located the water, the ladies'-room door had shuddered and closed behind the woman. Lydia remained at the basin, where she applied frosted peach lipstick with dripping hands, threw away the tube of lipstick and wiped her hands on her dress.

Lydia approached the bench in the courtyard next to the fountain that looked like a gigantic rubber-band ball, where Franklin chatted with the woman in red. Their shoulders touched as they laughed, and an air of intimacy pervaded, as obvious and overwhelming as the syrupy scent of night-flowering jasmine. "You were right, darling," he said when Lydia joined them, as he handed her champagne, in a real glass flute this time. "I was smiling at this woman earlier. I didn't realize that I recognized her, but I did. We're old friends. Janice, meet Lydia. Lydia, Janice."

"Old, old friends." Janice smiled her awful smile. "Franklin was just telling me how you met."

"Yes," said Lydia, stupidly.

"It sounds thrilling," said the too-red lips.

"We've waited a whole year for *The Rite of Spring*. And if we're going to get into those orchestra seats this time, we should be going." Franklin grinned and slid his hand down the length of his silk tie, flipping up the end with a flourish.

"The idea of The Rite of Spring *came to me while I was still composing* Firebird," *Igor Stravinsky recalled, 45 years after the ballet's first performance in 1913. "I had dreamed of a scene of pagan ritual in which a chosen sacrificial virgin danced herself to death."* Franklin had secured the second-row seats as promised. While he chatted up the usher about the use of material on the grantors' wall, Lydia slipped by, then pretended to need assistance removing her wrap. Now, head down, studying her program, heart percussing wildly in her chest, throat, and ears, Lydia found herself reading the same sentences over and over. All she could think of were the words she had put in that woman's—Janice? Janet?—mouth: "Does Franklin still swing?" "Does he still take those crazy photographs?" *The evocative opening, with the bassoon playing in its highest register, immediately transports the listener to some vague, primeval past as Stravinsky conjures what he described as "a sort of pagan cry."*

The music crashed and thundered with jarring percussion and offbeat rhythms. Lydia's mind leapt to one possible future. Some Saturday afternoon, with her husband Franklin out returning videos and Lydia home in her pajamas, holding a fan of glossy Polaroids of anonymous body parts, red, shiny, engorged; opened and spread by manicured fingers, wrists with gold watches. Quick! What kind of watch did Franklin wear? A brown leather band. Was it cracked? Crocodile? A gold face. She really had no idea and was more ashamed for not knowing the kind of watch her husband wore than she was for going through the photos in the manila envelope that she'd imagined she'd found in the drawer behind his shorts.

Franklin had a right to his sex life before he met her, of course he did. They were adults! But these! She studied each photo carefully, dreading the next for fear that he'd be there, her Franklin, naked but for a pointy party hat and those dumb sport socks he favored, surrounded by a harem of housewives, nuzzling his neck or energetically bouncing their heads above his cock. Lydia might understand if they were beautiful women, models or porn stars or strippers or whores, who represented fantasies that Lydia herself could never achieve. Would never even *want to* achieve! But to think that Franklin partied with—was that the proper term?— "swung" with regular people like themselves, was unfathomable to Lydia. She imagined a PTA meeting of parents and teachers, then removed all their clothes, put gin and reefer into their hands, and watched as they screeched and howled and paired off in groups of twos and threes to grunt and moan and spill drinks and burn holes in bad orange carpeting. For some reason, they always wore hats and shoes; she could never make them all the way naked.

She held her breath as she flipped to the next photograph, and because it was her fantasy, her worst nightmare came true. Here were Franklin and Janice/Janet, not just together, not just naked, not just wearing hats and shoes and drinking cocktails from Dixie cups, wearing cracked, brown leather watches and too-red lipstick, not just ignoring receding hairlines and long teeth, saggy, lopsided breasts and stretch marks, heat rashes from thigh rubbing and carpet burns, but holding hands, dammit!, and smiling.

The music was wild and stark. She peeked at Franklin and was surprised when she found him watching her and smiling. She laid her head on his shoulder and, through her lashes, searched for Alistair's toupee, her beacon, in the row far above the orchestra where they had sat during the first half. She imagined a woman in a wooded glade, encircled by bears and other beasts; dancing, dancing, dancing, until she dropped.

The End

GARDENLAND

THE SILVER DRESS WAS PERFECT. It showed off Chichi's still fine tits and camo'd the spray of blue veins above the backs of her knees. She turned off the overhead light and lit some candles, then sat on the closed lid of the toilet just like her mother used to do. She'd been thinking a lot about her mother. Candlelight rippled against the turquoise and lavender tiles, transforming the small Spanish-style bathroom into a kind of nighttime aquarium. She inhaled the last of the lines from her hand mirror, then propped it up to start on her eyes. The phone rang and she only half-listened as Phil left a slurred message. "Baby, you almost ready? You're over an hour late and everyone's already sloshed. I know you don't want to miss your favorite bubbly on your big five-oh. You must be on your way. I'll try the cell."

Chichi's body had always been dynamite, but her eyes, she knew, were her best feature. It took more time to cover the lines now, more glitter to bring out the sparkle of her faded blues. Phil was a sweetheart. Getting their friends together, renting the room, calling in favors to get a case of her favorite champagne. Her official birthday wasn't until Sunday but tonight, Friday night, was her party. Fifty fucking years old; twenty-five since she'd seen her mama. Chichi wondered what that might be like.

She imagined a garden hose coiled under a dripping faucet, its line snaked across a patch of rusty summer lawn, hissing spray. White plastic porch furniture, one chair pulled away, perfect for lounging on an early June Sacramento night. Mama would be turned out in a yellow sweater set and slacks, hair washed and feet bare, toes painted coral. She'd hold a glass of lemonade in one hand, a bowl of sugar in the other; and when she saw Chichi she'd likely let loose a scream. The lemonade might spill and the sugar bowl drop. They'd bend down to clean it up together, laughing over the sweet, sticky mess. After not seeing each other for so long, there would be words—of course there would be words. Only Chichi could never imagine them. She never pictured the inside of her mama's house either, only its flat beige exterior, soothing and dull. Suddenly, she had to find out.

Dear Phil, she thought, I am sorry, but *I am going to have to miss my own party.*

Chichi packed a small bag; she wouldn't need much. But she did need a gift. Mama deserved something after all this time. In the place of honor on Chichi's stereo cabinet, under the light, was a small gold crown in a glass cube, dotted with jade and ruby chips. A gift from Phil after he took photos of her the first time. He was driving her back to her apartment in his pale blue Gran Torino when they stopped at Norm's for fried eggs and pie. His swimming pool eyes promised her so many things: her photo on calendars, postcards, placemats, refrigerator magnets, magazine spreads, some of which had mostly come true. "From Thailand," Phil said when he placed the crown in her hands, and the newly-legal Chichi had thrilled at the exotic link. After they finished the pie, he drove her to the university campus, where they parked atop of Structure B to gaze at the goldfish sunset. She took off her shirt and Phil took more photos of her right there in his car. He screeched like a predatory bird when he came.

Chichi wrapped the crown in a clean dishtowel, stowed it in her bag, and took a good look around her apartment. *No matter what happens,* she thought, *when I come back, everything will be different.* She didn't bother to change her clothes.

★   ★   ★

Chichi sat across from Marilyn Monroe's lipstick-smudged drawer at Westwood Village Memorial Cemetery, her yearly ritual around the day of their birth, June first. A threesome of crows landed on the lawn near her feet. They cawed loudly, heaving breasts so black they pearled platinum in the moonlight. One brazen little fuck hopped close to peck at Chichi's brown paper sack. Chichi took the bottle of wine from the sack, screwed open the cap, and tossed back a ladylike slug. She held the wine in her mouth as she flattened the wrinkles from the brown paper and searched for a pen at the bottom of her purse.

Dear MM: My Big Five-Oh. Can you believe it? Ducking out on my own party. I love it. I doubt the fools will even miss me. As for last year's promises, I haven't done a line in over 3 months until tonight but if I hadn't, I wouldn't have realized I spent half my life away from home and now it's time to go back. I'd be lying if I said I wasn't twitchy about it—you never know what that woman might do when she sees me. And who knows what the hell I'll say to her. But this is my dream. You always tried to be true to yours, no matter how hard the world came down on you. I think of you, my inspiration, and how much we're the same, just always needing more love. Eternally yours, C.

Chichi reread the letter a few times to herself, pretending one time to be Marilyn and finding herself touched and pleased once she scratched out the last line, which she decided was too obvious and sad. Then she rolled the paper up into a ball, lit a cigarette and watched the words sink into themselves and disappear.

★   ★   ★

Chichi loved driving up the long deserted Interstate and let her silver-blonde hair whip out the side window like a horse's tail. She found herself lost in sensual reveries—the mix of fear and excitement when she went home with strange men, getting mugged at knife point one night in Hollywood, the sound of her

71

pinky finger snapping when she had to break into her own apartment—only to wake up, suddenly alert and driving through all of them. She was amazed when this happened, that she managed to stay inside the lines and not plow into anyone while her mind was so far away. She wondered how her mama really was, acknowledging the sweater set/sugar bowl scenario was nowhere near true.

Over the years, Chichi had called home just to hear her voice. She called at different times of day to gauge the drinking. From different phones—pay phones at laundromats, mobile phones, house phones at parties of people she hardly knew—to make sure her mama wouldn't black out Chichi's calls or whatever people do when they don't want to hear from someone. Usually Chichi hung up right after Hello, but sometimes she waited, listening to her mama's breath, or her long snapping inhale on a More or Newport. Sometimes she listened to the background TV, hysterical sitcom laughter or the screak of game show applause. Once her mama must have forgot to hang up or the receiver slipped from the cradle or the cell phone button didn't get pushed the right way. Chichi fell asleep listening to her mama's sighs, an occasional grunt as she heaved up or down into the sofa, the click-clack of a dog's toenails on linoleum, crackling candy bar wrappers. It was so soothing when no one was flapping their jaws.

Chichi jangled with anxiety as soon as she hit the stretch of the Interstate where the 5, 99 and 16 became one. She gripped the steering wheel as she crossed over Discovery Park, with its new duck-filled river, which was just an old cement drainage canal when she was a girl, and thickets of fresh trees. To the east, downtown Sacramento's skyline was a length of amber lights, much vaster than she'd ever seen. But as soon as she exited onto the El Camino Road, everything in the old Gardenland neighborhood looked just as Chichi remembered. Small houses sat far back from the street with long lawns and tall trees, some thick with fruit, surrounded by strict cyclone fences.

Mama's block was quiet and Chichi cut the engine before pulling up in front of her place. The house was still beige. It matched the dead lawn. Chichi started to get out of the car, but caught herself. She couldn't go knocking on Mama's door at two o'clock in the morning. Instinctively, Chichi made her way to the local main drag, now a wide boulevard almost unrecognizable. She'd stop for a bite, some coffee, maybe a line. She passed one chain restaurant after another as she drove through the Gateway Plaza, a new Gardenland development among many, until she came to a small one-story place at a back corner location. The Wagon Wheel diner, where she and her ex-husband Vince used to devour post-party pancakes at 3 a.m., advertised wine spritzer margaritas. Butterflies burned in Chichi's stomach as she steered her car towards the wooden arrow. The trees in the parking lot had been spindly and new back in the day. Now, the sallow green of their scant canopy and tumor-knobbed trunks left her feeling unmoored. She crossed the asphalt as though she were entering a memory that wasn't fully her own.

The bell tinkled on the heavy glass door and her silver sandals made sharp, tearing sounds on the sticky linoleum. There was no hostess; the place was deserted. Chichi headed toward the back, past a long bank of windows covered with dark film that cast a milky purple glow on the orange booths and amber panes of glass that divided them. As she pushed open the door under the sign that said "Gals," a woman's husky laugh burst from the kitchen.

Chichi washed her hands and studied her face in the mirror. Her eyes were still young, she decided. She checked out her profile, her ass, adjusted her tits, smoothed her long silver dress. Having lived half her life in Los Angeles, she had developed a certain city style, and would never be considered a gal. When Chichi came out of the ladies room, the hostess was waiting.

"Sorry 'bout that. Had my hands full," she said, straightening her hair and winking at someone over Chichi's shoulder. "Let's get you seated. Would you like to sit at the counter?"

This one's a gal, Chichi thought. Good curves, fair skin, a fresh piece of gum by the looks of her hard-working jaw. Younger than Chichi, but not as sexy. *No fuckin' way.* "I'll take this booth," Chichi said, slipping into one in the middle of the room.

"No can do. Booths are reserved for parties of four," the gal chirped, blinking her robin's egg blue lids.

"Are you shitting me?" Chichi looked around, still the only customer. "Your shirt's on inside-out."

A man's voice snorted behind the open kitchen counter as the hostess inspected her side seams and looked down the front of her blouse. "Oh my goodness," she said. "I was in such a rush…"

"Whatever." Chichi opened the menu, then without reading it, flung it back at the hostess. "Give me a half-stack of silver dollars, with strawberry syrup, not maple, lots of butter, skip the sugar, three strips of bacon, hot coffee and cold OJ." She could recite it in her sleep.

The hostess took Chichi's ticket back to the counter and said something in a low voice. The man laughed louder this time, a deep chuckle.

"Who's that?" Chichi asked when the hostess came back with her coffee.

"He's our Executive Chef and he's going to whip up something special just for you." Her smile suggested she knew what she was talking about.

Chichi dumped three packets of NutraSweet in her cup—two more than normal. She sensed him with her entire body, every hair on alert from the back of her neck to the V of her crotch, sensation flooding her brain, her skull trembling with the light and rush of him. Her hands clenched into fists, rough-bitten nails digging into her palms. Executive Chef at the friggin' Wagon Wheel. *Jesus H.*

The first time he came to her house to ask her out, she slammed the door in his face with a death threat. But their first date, God that car—white leather seats and a stampeding engine, burning donut rings in the parking lot at the shopping mall with her hands between his legs and her tongue in his ear. She swore she'd never marry him no matter how much he begged, but he begged just enough and she surrendered. He was an animal and she became one when she was with him.

He laughed as he helped the hostess take off her blouse to turn it the right way out, then murmured in that way that he had. Chichi pricked her ears to hear that piece of shit's voice—the croon of meaningless promises that flew like swallows from his red velvet tongue. She'd done her time chasing after those birds, holding crumbs in her open hands while they hopped this way and that.

When Chichi looked up he was there, all of him, and so much of him was so much the same. The impudent slope of his shoulders, the Gothic lettering on his faded black t-shirt, the way he stood legs spread wide, like his nuts were too big to do else wise.

"Well, looky here," he said. He tongued a toothpick from one corner of his cat's canary smile to the other, taking her in with his breath, with his thighs. "Patricia."

His hands seemed to sprout from the ends of his arms like heavy fruit. Amazing how delicate those huge hands could be. During the almost-year they were married, Chichi watched Vince thread needles to sew her name in his palm, clean pipe filters, roll scores of dollar bills for snorting and countless perfect joints. His thick fingers caressed cigarettes galore and she'd get wet just watching the guy flick his Bic, shattered by the tiny orange flame cupped in his cavernous palm. She thought the divorce cured her, but here she was, practically jizzing her pants. She would say hello, she swore to God, that was all. But her hands drifted lazily above her head to drape her hair around both sides of her face, as though shaping an imminent embrace, lifting the low-cut part of her silver dress, as though Vince were a camera, her life spent in front of the lens insisting she find just the right trick of light, that she push one shoulder back just so. "I go by Chichi now," she drawled, willing herself not to say more, to refrain from one inviting word, one seductive gesture.

He slid into her booth and pushed her plate across the table. "Chichi. I like the sound of that. What you been up ta?" His smile was threatening and familiar.

Chichi drenched a forkful of pancakes in syrup, swirled it through the whipped butter, then raised the dripping fork to her lips. She closed her eyes and chewed slowly, humming at the sweetness in her mouth, promising herself, *only Hello*. Even then she could feel him raking her like a wolf on a flock of spring lambs. She knew how much he loved to watch her eat.

"Place looks different," she said, looking around at his bachelor trailer.

"That's 'cause Pop ain't asleep in the corner," Vince nodded in the direction of the chair in front of the television. "He died about five years ago."

"I'm sorry," Chichi said. "Your pop was always nice to me."

"Boys were always nice to you." Vince laughed and bumped her with his hip, pushing her over onto his rumpled bed. "That was easy."

She felt instantly at home. "Honey, I was born easy."

"Except when we were married." He threw himself down next to her and cracked a couple cans of beer. "You look the same too," he said. "That teenage girl body with the porn star parts. That's some dress."

"Yeah, right," she said, sipping, privately pleased. "I look better in the dark."

"We'll see about that. Close your eyes."

She shivered as he pushed up her dress; she knew what was next. His lips took a wayward path down her stomach. She kept her eyes shut tight, picturing his big head on cement blocks in front of the trailer. She'd keep it company with her Jack & Coke, close to the curb, letting the sun redden her shoulders. She'd light its giant cigarette. She could do anything she wanted with her eyes closed.

"Tell me what's been going on." His moist finger entered her mouth, rubbed her gums, then rubbed some more down inside her.

"Vince, I don't do that anymore," she murmured, but already she liked where she was headed.

"Don't do what?"

He rubbed more powder on her lips, worked his hand like a bird. Fluttering, flying. She remembered now, what it was like to be with him, comforting as a bruise, convincing as a slap on the face. Her legs scissored like chopsticks. "Fuck, Vince!" she cried.

"That's my girl!" He laughed and wrapped her legs behind him. "You want it. Tell me."

"I want it," she said, wondering how she remembered the words, the position. She was born this way. Born from him. "Of course I want it." Floating around in her head was how she wanted it. Floating where the dead were not dead. It was only a matter of time before they wrapped her thoughts, eclipsing the light. All she ever wanted was light.

He slapped her belly. "Don't fall asleep on me, doll."

She opened her eyes and saw him looking up at her, framed between her legs. She guffawed. "You could be my baby. Just like that. You could."

"Don't get sick on me. I'll stop. I swear I'll stop."

"No. Don't ever stop." They'd been in his trailer ever since he clocked out. But tomorrow was her birthday, and Chichi was in Sacramento, and Vince was going with her to visit Mama. A girl could do worse, and she had.

"I'm hungry," he said. "We been in here for hours."

"Ever since you watched me eat breakfast." She grinned.

"I'll be back," he said, stepping into black slacks, buttoning up his bowling style shirt with the orange flames burning at the hem. "I need to make a quick run for beer, tacos, cigarettes…" He ticked off his fingers.

"I quit," she said.

"Good for you. Some flowers for your ma." He winked. "A birthday present for someone."

As Chichi scraped hardened pizza crusts into the trash, her brain swam with visions like glittering coins. Vince could get her pictures on calendars and placemats, get her that magazine spread Phil had never been able to score. She hummed as she wiped down the fronts of the cabinet doors, folded blankets and sheets ringed with stains of God-knew-what, stowed dirty pots and pans in the miniature oven and shoved his dirty clothes under the bed, stubbornly ignoring the clock.

An hour passed, then two, then it was Saturday night. He must have run into some friends and lost track of time, she thought. She brought her duffel bag from her car and took an uncomfortably cramped shower, then put her silver party dress back on just to remind him of what he'd been missing. By the time she put up her hair and glued on her eyelashes, she was worried and itching for a smoke. When Chichi knocked on the window of the neighboring trailer, wouldn't you know the most beautiful man she'd ever seen would have to go and open the door.

★ ★ ★

If motherfucker Vince had been at that party, he wouldn't have let her drive. He would have buckled Chichi in the front seat and driven home slow, the back way, where there were no lights, no cops, no time for illusions. But motherfucker Vince wasn't there, hadn't even returned from the convenience store yet. The night had belonged to Chichi and the beautiful man, except beautiful man had gone back to the trailer park hours ago, and Chichi'd stayed with the guy with the shit, the smokehouse guy, the guy with the throaty laugh who made her feel meaningless and destructive.

It was hours before Chichi realized she had no wheels, no way to get back to Vince's trailer. The smokehouse guy had disappeared too. There was a locked door with loud voices behind it, but Chichi didn't want to bother with that. Anyway, she was mostly sober. Rain was just beginning to spit down as she tiptoed to the curb, a shoe on each shoulder. Her mouth tasted of chalk and pizza and the night jiggled lightly around her as she deliberately forgot the guy's one-syllable name and ridiculously dainty hands. She looked at the cars parked up and down the street. Most people left their cars unlocked in these parts; the truck would be the easiest to steal.

She pulled the wires down from under the dash and crossed them like her brother taught her when she was fourteen. She was soaked by the time she settled herself behind the wheel; her silver dress was now a botch of pure black. She could do this. It was only two miles. How long could it take? Seventeen miles an hour—shit—seventeen divided by a mile times sixty. She laughed. At this rate, she'd make it there by yesterday. She turned on the radio. Something country to soothe her raving breast. Steel guitar sounded like heart strings, motherfucker always said. *Goddamn romantic.*

The big Ford's engine rumbled to life. Chichi thrilled at the power of the accelerator under her bare foot. Alone on the road, she made it to the light at the end of the block without forgetting to stop, its one cherry eye beaming like vampire blood. *There. Fine.* The windshield wipers slappity slap, tossing fine spray, a momentary clearing before her vision puddled with rain again. It was so beautiful and dark around her, she could almost hear the quiet town breathe, could feel the streets rise like a man's belly in sleep. Men's bellies were so beautiful, the dark trail of hairs curling up like moss from between their beautiful legs with their beautiful cocks, slappity slap. A car was honking behind her now and she decided to think it was beautiful too, a message of love between two machines, a gesture of recognition in the dense black night. The car honked again and its impatient driver swerved around her to the left. Chichi looked for the light, the light, to tell her to go, or to stay in beauty, but there was none, just darkness, dark dark, like the insides of your eyes with the kaleidoscope of blood. Dark like a blindfold, or inside the bad closet. Dark like home in a country boy's heart, and she dug in her purse for a cigarette while she waited for the light, then laughed when she remembered she'd quit. Then somewhere outside someone started to yell, and she panicked, accelerating in a beautiful rush of speed and sound, drawn forward by magnets and inner strength, into the darkness, the beautiful dark. There was no way she could have seen him until he ran right in front of her, waving his arms, chasing who knows what, demons? Black, darkling butterflies? It was as though he flew straight into her and she saw him only on impact, his beautiful bloodied face.

★　　★　　★

You could scrub as hard as you wanted with that Fels Naptha granny-ass soap, wax paper wrapped, scent like a sharp stick up your nose—but it never lathered up luxurious and creamy like Dove. Fels Naptha was the Brillo of soap, its lather a barking growl that removed your skin with the dirt.

Chichi washed her hands until they shone pink, then scoured her feet with a lather like broken cement. Skin sloughed off in yellow, calloused layers. She'd gone barefoot since she was practically twelve. But that was a long time ago. I may be an old bitch, she thought, but my feet are baby-soft.

She kindled up another handful of thin, unsatisfying grit and looked in the mirror. Her whole damn face was a map of her life anyway. The stitch at the end of her left eyebrow. Always been a bump there since the cut got infected. Such a prominent ridged scar for such a small tear, and it pulled up her brow so she looked Chinese on one side. Vince used to call it her Mexican facelift, her Tijuana Tuck. But she hated her face now and didn't have the presence of mind to blame the cheap, ruined glass. She draped Vince's old Ronrico Rum t-shirt over it. She didn't want to study what she saw. Didn't want to know if she had changed or if what she had seen was true.

The boy could be alive. He could certainly be alive. It was hard to say whether he had jumped off the hood of her truck or slid off as she drove away. She wanted to go back. Had a whole argument with herself about it, arguing still as she pulled into the trailer park and saw Vince had not yet returned. But she won the argument and decided to stay. Or had she lost?

Her neck ached from snaking forward and back when she slammed on the brakes. Ah, she'd be fine. Whiplash was for pussies. She'd survived worse. She was waiting for him now. Again. Still. Reading his Ronrico Rum t-shirt backwards as she brushed her teeth. Turned the shirt inside out and read it some more. muR ocirnoR. Reminded her of *Murder, She Wrote*. The thought made her shiver and she splashed her face with rank water. Five times. Twenty five. Every time new. Every time clean. But not clean enough. She lathered up again, up to her elbows, like fancy dress gloves you'd wear to a Cinderella ball. Wandered around the house in her Fels Naptha gloves, made of the finest Corinthian Lather. Shit, now *that* was funny. Hoped she'd remember it so she could tell Vince. She missed her chablis, but she vowed to quit everything. Smoking. Wine. Vince. Waiting. She thought about just getting in her car and going on without him, but it was too long since she'd seen him, and what happened last night made her scared.

She squeezed her eyes shut and pretended she was blind. Took two babyfresh steps to the left into the crumbly foam mattress. Right, right. This was easy. Two steps forward and she was in the kitchenette. Yes, yes. She stood at the small sink in her long, lather gloves, posing like Marilyn. One hand shading the Chinese eye like Phil taught her during late afternoon shoots; the other poised at the end of her long, graceful arm, waiting for a glass of chablis, not champagne.

"Hey doll." It was Vince. He'd come in quiet like summer, his voice soft rain and crickets, delicious tobacco in the wreath of his hair.

"Shit! You scared me!" Her hand fell to her side.

"I brought flowers," he said, as he took down a cookie jar shaped like a pig. "You cleaned up." He kissed her cheek. "A woman's touch sure makes a difference."

Chichi took three steps sideways into the dinette, lost in her reverie, wondering how to correct the spin. When his eyes met hers, she would turn her hand over and present him her palm, like a kitten's belly. He'd fall for it and she'd surprise him with a quick slap. She wanted to see the print of her hand on his face, the quick hurt surprise in his eyes, yes, the hurt always made her wet. She found a pack of cards, dealt herself a game of Solitaire. Just to keep focused, impartial.

Vince filled the jar with water, toweled off the drips, fluffed the daisies, and set them in the center of the small table before he pulled two packs of Marlboro from his pocket. He stripped one of its plastic, ripped open the foil interior with his teeth, and offered her a cigarette.

She leaned forward and touched her hand lightly to his as he cupped the match. "What happened?" she asked. She had a right to know, didn't she?

"I slept with Shammi last night. Accidentally." So matter of fact, as though he'd said *I'll be back*.

"What do you mean 'accidentally?' Did you drive into her?" Chichi inhaled half the cigarette, felt its nicotine treat blast her brain, fuel her heart. Fuck quitting. She watched the blossoming ash, the paper blackening and crackling behind it. She embroidered her name in the air with smoke, dotted the I's with two stabs of her fingers. She'd quit everything later, just not now.

"You know what I mean." He dropped his lazy lids over eyes the color of kerosene. "Let's not have no dogfight about it."

Chichi pretended to study the cards. The Queen of Hearts was going to get it on with the King of Spades. Big deal. Vince had sex with the ex. Chichi was the ex, too. And he was here now, right? With her, dig? They smoked together silently in a Mexican standoff.

Finally Vince ground his filter onto the ceramic pig, then stood up to shrug off his light blue jacket. He winged his arms out of his webbed suspenders, letting them hang down from his waistband like garters. He kicked off his blue and white loafers, peeled off shiny nylon socks, then rolled up the cuff of his light blue pants.

Chichi slid the king to her queen. "Weren't you wearing something else when you left?"

"Yes, ma'am. Shammi felt like doing a little shopping." He plopped down on the foam cushion next to her, wriggling his toes in the air. "You like?"

She looked him up and down, as though noticing him for the very first time, which she wasn't but it felt like that anyway, except they weren't in The Wagon Wheel where everything started. Again. They were in Gardenland Mobile Home & RV Park. "You look like the frigging Easter pimp."

"The what?" His head swiveled at her. His eyes bulged out and his mouth hung open. She could see all the gold molars in the back, five of them. Money in the bank, he called them.

"You heard me," she said, finally pulling the seven that was the key to the game, to everything, one card slapping quickly on top of another now, four little piles triumphant at the top of the table, slap, slap, slap, slap! Royalty, one after the other.

"Why you don't got no clothes on?" he asked, lolling back on the futon, crooking his pinky at her and patting the space next to him, lazing that enchilada hand of his all along his crotch.

Chichi lit a new cigarette off her old one, then balanced it on the edge of the table where she hoped it would melt the ugly

Formica top, maybe torch the whole freakin' trailer park. She lay down next to Vince, tears in her eyes. She would tell him about the accident, but first she had to get him ready. She opened her mouth and he kissed her.

"I'm not feeling it, doll."

She ground into him rhythmically.

She.

Would.

Tell.

Him.

But not now. Tomorrow. Soon. What did it matter when, if they were going to be together for eternity?

★   ★   ★

Sunday. Chichi's Big Five-Oh was today—she could hardly believe it. Vince gave her a hell of a good-morning screw, but didn't seem to be in any big hurry to get on the road to Mama's. When he lit out for coffee, Chichi packed up her bag, grabbed the extra pack of cigarettes, and drove her car back to the street where it happened. She went during daylight, on her big day. Somehow it felt braver, like more of a punishment. She sat on the curb and smoked until the cigarettes were gone, then cried until her feet were damp with tears. A couple of teenage boys stood right where it happened, as though the dead or maybe not dead boy had melted into the soil and from his mess had sprung two brand-new boys. They wore crew necks, extra long shorts and knee-high athletic socks. Must be some kind of a church made them dress that way. There was one skateboard between them, and they alternated throwing it down on the street, hopping on it, and falling onto a patch of dried grass. One of them spray-painted something on the long cinder block wall, pointed at Chichi and laughed. BITH, he had written, in voluptuous pussy-pink letters. "You spelled it wrong, peckerhead," Chichi yelled after the boys as they laughed like dogs and ran down the street, pushing each other into walls, bushes, parked cars.

She stood and brushed off her bottom, which ached from her long sit on cement. She kicked off her flip-flops and clomped barefoot to an abandoned gas station. She squeezed through a slash in the chainlink fence and headed toward the back of the small outbuilding, where a massive tropical vine had taken root and grown wild. Fuchsia blooms as big as her fists covered one wall up to the roof. An insane chirping came from somewhere below. Baby birds, throats open, gasping and calling. It made her sick.

It was close to lunchtime now. Her mama was probably asleep. There was still time—there was still the whole rest of her day—so Chichi went back to the trailer to wait. She sat on the little square porch, her purse on her lap, peeling off the flakes of green paint from the concrete pad that was supposed to be a patio, possibly a lanai. She'd tell off the bastard, then leave, with or without him. She hoped with. *What if it's all a dream anyway? What if everything is meaningless? And we're just plastic zoo animals and our words are alphabet magnets.*

She dug to the bottom of her purse. There was this one picture of her where she looked like a movie star, she really fucking did, and she automatically thought of Marilyn, the way her toe pointed, the shine on her cheek, biting her scarf. There used to be lots of photos of Chichi like that, but now there was only the one, dog-eared at the corners and burned a bit where she'd dozed off smoking while looking at it as she did from time to time. It wasn't her favorite; she'd always said the Lucite shoes took the spotlight away from her legs and you could almost see the lines of her cooch, but still. Someday she ought to frame it.

The End

Acknowledgments

Heartfelt thanks to Cathy Colman, Anna Cook, Mom, Pop & Jon De-Brincat, the Dordogne, the Hollywood sign, all the J's in the Kelly family, National Geographic, Carl Peel, Igor Stravinsky, 1592 Treat Avenue, Wednesday nights.